By Kathleen Karr

It Ain't Always Easy
Oh, Those Harper Girls!
Gideon and the Mummy Professor
The Cave
In the Kaiser's Clutch

IN THE
Kaiser's
Clutch

KATHLEEN KARR

IN THE
Kaiser's
Clutch

Farrar, Straus and Giroux
New York

Library of Congress Cataloging-in-Publication Data
Karr, Kathleen.
In the Kaiser's clutch / by Kathleen Karr.—1st ed.
p.   cm.
[1. Twins—Fiction. 2. Brothers and sisters—Fiction.
3. Single-parent family—Fiction. 4. Motion pictures—Production and
direction—Fiction. 5. World War, 1914–1918—United States—Fiction.]
I. Title.
PZ7.K149In   1995   [Fic]—dc20   94-44445 CIP AC

For Suzanne,
my favorite critic

IN THE
Kaiser's
Clutch

1

Caught in the Web

Fitzhugh and Nelly Dalton, All-American teen twins, find their privileged life of tennis and golf interrupted when a friend invites them to tour the German U-boat *Deutschmark* and they inadvertently stumble upon a nefarious scheme to bomb New York Harbor.
  —"This Week at the Serials," *Moving Picture World*

"Fitz, dear, *please*! This scenario has to be finished by afternoon."

Fitzhugh Dalton grudgingly stopped bouncing his tennis ball off the kitchen wall. "But, Ma, Nelly and I have to be on the movie set tomorrow morning. How can we do that tennis match you wrote for the serial if we've never hit a ball in our lives?"

Before Dorothy Dalton could answer, a small white missile arced through the open window of the crowded ground-floor apartment, narrowly missing her head. The golf ball made a hole-in-one in the blue enamel coffeepot atop the cast-iron stove.

Mrs. Dalton sighed, resettled wire-rimmed glasses on

her nose, and ripped a piece of coffee-splattered paper from her typewriter at the table. "Tell your sister she needn't practice her golf quite yet. That's for a later episode. As for you, tennis *outside*—at the corner park. Take Nelly with you. Tennis requires *two* players."

Grumbling, Fitz stuffed tennis balls in his pockets and picked up the racket. He brightened at a thought. "What's for dinner, Mother mine? Better yet, what's for lunch?"

"Nothing for either if I'm not paid. The icebox is empty, not to mention iceless. And I won't be paid if this episode of *In the Kaiser's Clutch* isn't ready on time." She glanced up from her typewriter again, thick brown hair slipping from its pile atop her head, and toyed absently with her earrings. "Do try to learn to hit the ball properly, dear. I swore to Pathmark Studios that you and Nelly would be perfect as their new serial stars. Five dollars a day for each of you, starting tomorrow. We'll be able to pay the rent, and get some ice, and . . ."

But Fitz had already departed. He jumped nimbly over the steps from the porch of the three-tiered white clapboard house, landing on the balls of his feet. Tall, lean, and very blond, white shirt collarless and open, and plaid flannel knickerbockers bagged stylishly over his knees, he did appear the image of privileged youth his mother was concocting. His twin sister, Nelly, was the female counterpart. At the moment she stood with a golf club poised for another disastrous swing. Her starched shirtwaist was crisp. Her navy cotton sports skirt was hiked by the gesture well above trim ankles and laced kid shoes. Her equally blond braid shone down her back in the late May

sun, while her blue eyes sparkled above a delicate nose
sprinkled with a handful of freckles as she considered
and—

"Nix. You're getting too dangerous for Ma, Nelly."

The club drooped. "Oh, pooh. I was just getting the
hang of it."

Fitz reached up to the porch for a second tennis racket.
"Come on, let's try and lob a few in the park. Ma said the
opening tennis shot should only last a few seconds. For
atmosphere. If we can manage to get the ball over a net
three times running, we're home free."

"What about this golf stuff?"

"Stash the lot in the hallway. Ma borrowed it from Mr.
Cedric Holmquist, the director, himself. We're in for it if
his equipment disappears."

Nelly complied, a frown forming on her heart-shaped
face. "I'm not convinced about this movie business, Fitz."
She accepted the second racket and swung down the
street after her brother. "What if we turn out horribly
unphotogenic? Some people are, you know. Then there
are all those ridiculous stunts we'll be expected to per-
form. And not just once, either, like in a proper feature
film, with a proper beginning and end. Our serial story
will just continue on in unfinished parts for fifteen
weeks—"

"I thought you were keen on acting."

Nelly struck a pose. "On the *legitimate* stage. Only the
finer works."

"Just because you played a few scenes from Shakespeare
at school last semester, you needn't put on airs. You're
not exactly Bernhardt or Duse yet."

"What airs?" Nelly deflated. "And screen acting *is* totally different. You can't talk, for one thing. For another—"

"Don't be such a nervous Nelly, Sis!"

The netting of her racket came down on his head with a thump, and Fitz jumped from further harm's way, thrusting out his own racket as a foil. *"En garde,* foul villain!"

"You're the villain. You know I hate it when you call me that!"

They fenced halfway down the block, to stop, hot and breathless.

"All right, I apologize. But seriously, Nell, what other choice have we? We're fifteen, old enough to be helping to support Mother. It takes a long time for articles to be accepted by posh magazines, and writing is what she can do. Scenarios are fast, and she'll get paid fast. I hope. In the meantime, there'll be our acting fees coming in."

"And just in time, with Dad's insurance money completely gone. But I miss New York. Fort Lee, New Jersey, is so . . . so . . ."

"Dull. I agree completely. But this is where the movie studios are. And it's only for the summer. Things go well, we'll be back in New York and school in the fall."

"Or looking for jobs as salesclerks at Macy's."

Fitz's expression became pained. "Never."

"You'd rather try the factories, brother dear?"

"Dad wouldn't have approved of either. You know he always meant for us to go to college."

Nell viciously kicked a stone from her path, oblivious to the truncated gasp of pain that greeted its landing in the copse of nearby trees. "Dad also assumed we'd always have three square meals a day. Then he went and got himself killed in that Black Tom disaster. We're on our own, Fitz."

They'd reached the small square of grass just past the trees at the end of the block. Fitz dug out a tennis ball. "Two years now come July. If I ever get my hands on the fiends that set off that explosion—" He smashed into the ball and watched as it flew over the edge of the cliffs of the Palisades nearby to disappear toward the Hudson River.

"Smart. Cedric Holmquist will probably deduct the cost of that ball from our first day's pay."

Fitz grimly reached into his knickers for another ball. "I still say it was sabotage. German provocateurs. And someday I'll find Dad's papers to prove it." He tossed the ball into the air. "Where I'd like to be now is in Europe, carrying a gun against the Kaiser. It's awful being too young to do anything really useful for the war effort."

"The summer of 1918 is going to be a long one," Nelly sighed in agreement.

As Fitz struck at the new tennis ball, a hulking, sinister figure, his face a grimace of pain and frustration, pulled his bruised head out of sight behind a broad old elm, then scuttled away through the trees edging the park.

"They're not identical twins!"

Cedric Holmquist enjoyed playing the part of director to the hilt. Scarlet ascot wound around his long neck, slouch hat at a rakish angle over one eye, he had Fitz and

Nelly lined up against a black backdrop the next morning, the sunlight streaming through the glass-paneled roof of the studio building illuminating their faces. He studied them through a lens caught around his neck on a cord, much as a jeweler might examine a gem.

"They *are* a boy and a girl, Mr. Holmquist. To be truly identical would be a biological impossibility." Dorothy Dalton was trying valiantly to save her children's jobs. "And they are quite similar—"

"Yes, of course. The boy's face is more masculine, squaring off as it does at the chin. Still, they both have that scattering of freckles, not to mention that dimple . . ."

Fitz grimaced involuntarily. *Cleft!* he wanted to scream. Then he swallowed his pique and swiped at his face. It was a hothouse under this glass ceiling. He hoped most of their scenes would be filmed outdoors.

"But I was expecting them to be more of a height."

"Fitz has shot up over the past few months." Mrs. Dalton inspected her son's extra five inches proudly. His father had been well over six foot, and Fitz seemed to be stretching for that height faster than she'd noticed. While there was Nelly, quite the petite young lady. Reaching for her handkerchief, Mrs. Dalton dabbed at an eye almost hidden by the gauzy veil of her straw hat. Her babies were growing up.

"Something wrong with you?" barked the director.

"Merely a mote of dust." The handkerchief was shoved out of sight. "The scenario was written for twins . . ."

"And where am I to find another set on the instant,"

replied Holmquist with unconcealed sarcasm. "All right, then." Letting the lens fall to his chest, he clapped his hands, turning completely businesslike. "Time is money. We have numerous scenes to shoot today, and Episode One must be in the can by the end of the week. The entire serial is scheduled to begin exhibition in late September. It has an anti-German theme, after all. God forbid we dally and the War end. Camera? Outside for the tennis shots!" He halted in mid-stride before following the cameraman. "Ernest? Where is that assistant?"

"Here, sir!" A very earnest young man bustled into view.

"Find a jar of greasepaint and some eye sticks for the Daltons, and instruct them on their proper usage. Total novices. A little sun or a spotlight on those innocent faces and they'd photograph like horrors."

"Miss Dalton!"

Nelly was backed into the shadowy corner of an outdoor set, wondering if her first day of making movies would ever be over. The tennis shots had gone on for eternity, and now this.

"Arm over your forehead in terror! Thusly, Miss Dalton." Cedric Holmquist's skinny neck arched back, Adam's apple throbbing free of the ascot; an arm thrust up, and his eyes opened impossibly wide. "There's a mad Hun creeping up on you, closer and closer. He has a knife in his hand and a leer on his face—"

"Are you sure my mother wrote this?"

"Miss Dalton!"

"Come on, Sis," Fitz hissed from next to the waiting camera and its bored operator. "This is the fourth take, the sun is going down, and I'm hungry. I'll be the creeping Hun." Fitz dropped to his knees, grabbed a nearby twig, and approached, brandishing his weapon menacingly. "You don't get it right this time, I swear I'll dispatch you personally."

Nelly widened her eyes, screamed, and flung her arm dramatically.

"Perfect! That's a take." Holmquist dropped his megaphone. "Too bad I can't use you for the Hun, too, young man. You were fairly convincing. But I suppose I'll have to hire an extra for those shots tomorrow." The director began striding off the set. "Six o'clock in the morning, Daltons. Be late and I'll dock you."

"Yes, sir."

The twins burst into the apartment in tandem.

"Food!"

"What is that extraordinary smell, Mother?"

"Roast beef," she said with a grin. "And it hasn't been *that* long since we've had meat."

Fitz had his nose in the oven already. "With potatoes and carrots and—"

"Calm down, Brother, and help set the table. See if you can find the napkins." Nelly glanced at her mother. "What's the occasion?"

"To celebrate work for all of us—fifteen weeks guaranteed! . . . All the way through the summer" was added dreamily as she shoved her glasses higher on her nose. "If we watch our pennies, there'll be enough to carry us through the entire winter. Enough for school fees, and uniforms, and books, and—"

"And a new pair of glasses for you, Mother," concluded Nelly.

"Not before we get Ma's good typewriter out of hock, Nell. The old clunker she traded it for is missing the 'e' and the 's.' A professional needs decent tools." Fitz studied his mother more closely. "And probably your ruby earrings from Dad, too. You haven't worn them for a while."

Nelly spun around. "Mother, you didn't really! Your best earrings at the pawnbroker's?"

Their mother shrugged as if it were of little import. Nelly knew differently, but decided it would be prudent to change the subject. "May we eat now? Fending off vile fiends is exhausting work."

Fitz took her cue. "We shoot the submarine scenes tomorrow, Ma. They were just doing atmosphere and close-ups on Nelly and me today. It gets a little confusing. Don't they ever photograph a story in the order it's written?"

Dish towel in hand, Mrs. Dalton was easing the roasting pan from the oven. "Apparently not, dear. It's all in bits and pieces, and then they splice them together for the finished movie." She transferred the beef to a platter and began carving it.

"D. W. Griffith himself used to work at our studio, did you know that, Mother?" Fitz snatched at a piece of meat barely sliced and popped it in his mouth. "Maybe a little on the rare side?"

Dorothy Dalton stared at the roast oozing blood. "I did

follow the directions in the recipe book, but possibly it went in a little late when I got sidetracked by Scene Thirty-one—"

"And the Gish sisters," added Nelly, frowning at her brother's comment behind his back. "The cameraman was talking about them today. 'Miss Lillian,' he called her. Just imagine me, treading through the same studio as *Lillian Gish,* the finest actress of the silver screen!"

"And melting under the same lights and heat." Fitz was trying for another morsel of the roast, even though it was underdone.

"Sit, both of you." Their mother placed a laden platter on the table. "Ready or not, it's being served. And I think grace is in order. We've much to be thankful for."

Fitz filled his plate after the prayer. "Wouldn't Dad be proud of us." He bit into an uncooked carrot and chewed it manfully. "He always believed in self-reliance."

"Perhaps a little too strongly," Dorothy Dalton observed.

"How do you mean that? About how he lived or how he died? What exactly was Daddy doing during the accident, Mother?"

Fitz tried to warn off his sister. "Nell—"

His mother stopped him. "It's all right, both of you. I've done with my grieving, and it's time to move forward." She caught her daughter's eyes.

"Your father died as he lived, looking for answers that would satisfy him. He always wanted to understand the answers before going to a higher authority." Mrs. Dalton paused, gathered her resources, and proceeded in as businesslike a manner as she was able.

"As you know, he was in charge of security at Black Tom Island's piers. He didn't like to worry me over his work, but I knew most of the munitions leaving New York for the Allied cause were stored and shipped from the terminal at Black Tom. Everyone knew. Tons and tons of highly flammable powder and shells and shrapnel bombs . . . Too many tons . . . The very afternoon of the accident he told me he'd soon have a story for me that would defy any fiction I could conceive."

"And then what happened, Mother?" Nelly whispered, her food forgotten.

"He mentioned he'd begun making some private notes, just in case. I've told you about that before . . . I asked, 'In case of what?' He only laughed, kissed me goodbye, and went off to work." A single tear slid down Dorothy Dalton's still young and pretty face. She stanched it with her linen napkin.

"And the notes were never found," Fitz continued the story. "Not in our New York home, and—"

"—definitely not at Black Tom," finished Nelly with a sniff of her own. "It was all blown up. With Daddy."

Silence hovered over the table until Fitz remembered he was still hungry. Their mother played with her own food, then suddenly looked up.

"Strange . . . I've just recalled something else that happened. I'd forgotten about it for almost two years. I wonder what brought it to mind now?"

"What—"

"—Mother?"

"Going through his clothes . . . after. I found the most curious slip of paper. It was in your father's hand, scribbled like a shopping list. I thought it *was* a shopping list and tossed it away in my grief. But somehow the words must have lodged in my memory . . ."

"Yes?" urged Fitz.

Their mother picked up her water glass and sipped, as if for strength to continue. "Only five words it was:

> *cigars*
> *eggs*
> *dumplings*
> *coal*
> *pencils*

But you know, it only now occurs to me: your father never smoked in his life."

A sharp noise came from under the open window next to their table, the sound of something hollow cracking against hard wood. Fitz jumped to his feet and shoved his head through the opening. "What the dickens!"

He hoisted his long body through the frame and tumbled out, disappearing into the darkness. Nelly and Mrs. Dalton raced to the window, but could see nothing. Nelly moved as if to follow her brother, but her mother held her back.

"What's the matter, Ma?"

"This isn't one of my scenarios, darling. Rash but daring girls only belong in the movies."

Fitz finally returned—through the door—huffing. "I chased the scoundrel clear down the block, but he got away from me in the trees by the park." He fell into his chair. "What's going on, anyway? Fort Lee is too genteel

for prowlers under porch windows. Some rogue was eavesdropping on us!"

Nelly hugged her arms to her body. The early morning
air was still cool as they stood by the river. She stifled a
yawn. None of them had slept very well last night after
discovering their intruder. Even bolting the windows
hadn't made them feel secure—more like trapped. Who
could have been eavesdropping on them? More impor-
tant, why? She stared at the huge black object floating on
the Hudson in the shadow of the Palisades, trying to wipe
out the unsettling thoughts. "That's a submarine?"

Fitz studied the barge topped with a superstructure of
painted cardboard. "Nobody said this was a big-budget
production, Nelly. All we've got to do is *pretend* it's a submarine. Holmquist and the cameraman will take care of
the rest."

With a shrug, Nelly transferred her attention to the
handful of other actors joining them today. They were all
shivering, too—even dapper Paul Panther, a genuine serial star who was to play their long-absent guardian,
finally returned home from foreign travels. Chatting with
Panther was Lloyd Wright, a dark-haired, fresh-faced
young man in his early twenties—wonderfully dashing
in uniform—who was acting the part of their friend and
confidant. According to the script, Lloyd was a lieutenant
in the United States Navy and had invited them on the
submarine tour.

Nelly had to keep reminding herself that while *In the
Kaiser's Clutch* was meant as a propaganda piece against a
Germany the United States was currently at war with, the

action was set in 1916, before the two countries were enemies. That accounted for the extras hired that morning
to pose as the *Deutschmark*'s German crew. Her eyes held
on them a long moment. They certainly were a raffish lot.

"Ooh, Fitz, just watch that extra over there, the one
nearest the gangplank—doesn't he look particularly devious and wicked?"

Fitz laughed. "Holmquist picked him to be your
fiendish Hun. Schmidt, I think he called himself. He's
even got a real German accent. Not that it'll make any
difference in a silent film." He stopped as the director
beckoned to them. "I think it's time to climb down that
conning tower. Not to worry, Sis. The rear side is nothing
but a regulation wooden ladder."

"And why should I be daunted by a real conning tower,
I'd like to know?"

"I was only thinking about your skirt . . ."

Nelly patted the dark serge of her walking suit, then
adjusted the collar of the jacket and glanced down to
make sure her special brooch was in place on her blouse.
She'd pinned on her father's small, silver Black Tom security badge for inspiration. "Just because Ma wouldn't let
me chase after that beast with you last night, don't for a
minute think I'm not capable of doing anything you are,
Fitzhugh Dalton!"

"Stow it. It's time to do some work."

Weary from being pursued around the fake submarine for
most of the day, the twins trooped home from the studio
expecting another cooked dinner. The stove, however,
was cold. Their mother, on the other hand, was hot

enough. She had a bright smile fixed on her face. She was also wrapped in unaccustomed aprons, even a scarf hiding her hair.

"What in the world's—"

"—going on, Mother?"

"What's going on is we're moving. Tonight. Mrs. Bernini had an opening on the second floor. Practically the entire floor, in fact."

"But—"

"No buts, Fitz. The rent will be a little higher, but so will the elevation. And we get three whole bedrooms. One for each of us." She bestowed her strained smile on Nelly. "Won't that be nice, dear? We won't have to share anymore. Not huge bedrooms, mind you, but private, nonetheless . . ."

Fitz bent to stretch an arm around his mother's shoulders. "We could've handled that snooper, Ma. You didn't have to—"

Mrs. Dalton pulled herself straight, the smile now gone. "I'm still in charge of the three of us, Fitz, and I refuse to live in fear. We're sleeping safely and well tonight. With the windows open."

"Couldn't we even have a glass of milk first?"

"Certainly. I've milk and beef sandwiches waiting in the new kitchen upstairs, Fitz. Grab something and cart it up."

"Yes, ma'am."

Fitz reached for an already stuffed suitcase and trudged out the door. Nelly, feeling less ambitious, grabbed the lightest thing she saw—her father's violin case. She turned toward the door, only to be stopped by a thought.

"Why didn't you pawn Daddy's violin instead of your Remington typewriter, Mother? You *need* the good typewriter."

Her mother rubbed dust from her cheek. She'd obviously gotten no writing done all that day. She'd probably been scrubbing Mrs. Bernini's second floor.

"You know how your father loved his music, dear. I just couldn't do it. And I thought someday you or Fitz might want to give it a try."

Nelly considered the violin case before shaking her head. "Music has never been my forte, Mother. You know that. Not Fitz's, either."

"Nevertheless."

Nevertheless. Nelly shook her head and carried the keepsake out the door. At the foot of the stairs she paused to shout, "I'm coming, Fitz. You'd better save some of those sandwiches for me. I'm the one who was tied up and covered with spiderwebs on that pseudo U-boat for two hours this afternoon!"

"Fake spiderwebs, sissy!" came floating down the staircase through an obviously stuffed mouth.

2

The Flood of Fury

Saved in the nick of time from the deadly bite of a giant tarantula through the heroic efforts of twin brother Fitzhugh, Nelly Dalton is slowly recovering in the garden of the Dalton mansion. Their fast friend, Lieutenant Lloyd Wright, and Paul Panther, their guardian, join the twins in a discussion aimed at solving the plot that has been uncovered. It is decided that real evidence must be procured before notifying the police. Nelly and Fitz must return to the German submarine to steal the sabotage plans they have spied.

—"This Week at the Serials," *Moving Picture World*

Sunday afternoon, it chose to rain. Fitz had his chair tilted against one side of the kitchen table, and his feet dangling out the second-floor window.

"You could at least put your socks on, Fitz." His mother's voice, edged with a slight note of distaste, drifted up from the manuscript she was editing across the table.

"We were supposed to go swimming this afternoon, Ma. This is the closest I can come to it. Besides, this big old apple tree out here hides all ten of my toes from the neighbors' prying eyes." He evocatively wiggled the toes in question, rustling a few damp leaves on the nearest branch. "It'll be nifty to reach out the window for an

apple when they're ripe, but I do miss direct access to the
porch."

"No one's keeping you off it, Fitz," Nelly pointed out
from her end of the table. "You're hogging all the breeze.
Do hand over Ma's script for Episode Two. It's my turn to
see what I'm getting into this week."

Fitz languidly fluttered the clipped papers at her.
"Some great times, Sis. Wait'll you get a load of Scene
Fifty-five. It's bound to add dimensions to your *legitimate*
theater experience."

Taking the bait, Nelly rapidly flipped through pages
to a sudden stop. There was silence, followed by a shriek.
"Ma! Ma, it's not fair! Why do *I* have to be immersed in
inky-black waters up to my neck?"

"It's a plot device, dear. When the Germans find you
back inside the submarine, padding your bosom with
their papers, they really do need to get rid of you. Stuffing
you into one of the ballast tanks and opening the flood
ports to water seemed like a perfectly logical solution to
me."

"Mother! You know what Cedric the Peacock is going
to do with that scene. He's going to stew me in those
waters for *hours* till he gets his pleasing effect. I'll be
wrinkled as a prune. My clothes will be ruined! Why
don't you put Fitz in the bloody ballast tank? Why—"

"Nelly, dear," her mother interrupted. "I do believe
working with those picture people has had a deleterious
effect on your vocabulary. You mustn't succumb to the
common assumption that movie actresses are ill bred—
or worse."

"Well said, Mother," Fitz chimed in.

Mrs. Dalton shot her son a scathing look before continuing. "Besides, Nelly, you know a movie audience has no interest in seeing a young man undergo the Terrors of the Damned. They're putting their money up front to watch a damsel in distress."

"That's not fair, either. Why should women have to do all the suffering? Why must we be considered the weaker sex?"

"Excellent questions, Nelly. Ones I've been trying to formulate answers to for some time." Dorothy Dalton reached for a small paring knife and jabbed at the point of her lead pencil. "Perhaps after we get the Vote—"

A sudden guffaw erupted from Fitz.

"Fitzhugh Aloysius Dalton! I've not bred and raised you to be anti-Vote!"

Fitz sprang upright in his chair and banged his head on the hard upper slat. "I'm not anti-Vote, Mother. Far from it." He rubbed at the back of his head ruefully. "But President Wilson doesn't want to promote anything except his peace plan right now. There's no way he's going to push for the Women's Vote until after the War." Fitz pulled his feet inside. "And if you're so bothered by this women's rights business, Ma, why are you making Nelly's role in our serial so trite?"

"Because that's what the studio pays for. Any sort of damsel-in-distress story will do—so long as it has a war theme. Pathmark's management is very anxious to advance the war effort. Patriotism is currently big at the box office." Her pencil now shaved to a nub, Mrs. Dalton poked it at the papers in front of her with passion. The lead broke. "What I'm working on right here, on my day of rest . . . what I'm trying to work on"—she paused to give them both the eye—"is a feature-length drama based on the tribulations of the very suffragists who camped before the White House last year, trying to make the President see the light. *My Mama's in Jail for the Vote.* Told through a lovely, lonely, innocent child's point of view, it has humor, and pathos, and righteousness—"

"Ah, but will it sell?"

"Young man, time before the camera seems to be affecting you adversely, as well. You're becoming entirely too cocky. You may retire to your room until you remember who you are, and how old you are."

"Aw, Ma, I didn't mean anything. It's just that there's nothing to do—"

"Except needle your sister and me."

"Why don't you try Dad's violin if you're that bored, Fitz."

"I'm not that bored, Nelly."

Fitz slunk out of the kitchen and peace descended upon the table.

It was pouring Monday morning.

"Indoor shots today, cast," boomed Holmquist.

He needn't shout, Nelly thought to herself. It wasn't that large a cast. Just themselves, and Paul Panther and Lloyd Wright sipping coffee off to one side, both looking as if they'd had exhausting weekends. Lloyd had probably been off dancing till all hours with that ingenue who'd been throwing herself at him. Nelly sniffed. The female in question wasn't more than two or three years her senior—

Holmquist boomed once more. Nelly's head jerked back. Then again, maybe the decibel level went with the director's chosen persona for the day—totally unnecessary dark glasses shoved atop his head, and a white silk aviator's scarf wrapped dashingly around his neck. The flamboyant, daring look. One end of the scarf flapped as the director pivoted in the center of the room, stacked with painted scenes.

"Huns front and center!"

"Sir." It was Schmidt, appearing from nowhere. "I stand here."

"Where are the others?"

Schmidt stolidly wrung water from his soft cloth cap while rain beat a steady tattoo on the glass roof overhead. A vivid scar on his left cheek twitched. "The wet is very . . . wet."

"A little stormy weather and they've all scarpered off. Right, then. You've just been promoted to Head Hun. Stick around."

If he was pleased by the promotion, Schmidt showed little sign. He merely ran a hand through the dark stubble of his close-cropped hair and merged his thick body into the camouflage of the jungle scene behind him.

Holmquist took only another minute to consider before barking orders to hovering stagehands. "Make sure the small water tank is filled. We'll start with Scene Fifty-five."

Nelly groaned. Such a perfect morning for a watery death.

Someone in Costume had come up with a modest bathing uniform for Nelly, so at least her favorite dress was still intact. That was more than could be said for the rest of her. Nelly grimaced under the glare of the single spotlight that had been focused on her face from the chin up for past eons. She could feel the thickly layered greasepaint on her cheeks almost begin to sizzle from the heat.

"God save me from amateurs! Not a *grimace,* Miss Dalton. It is not disgust which we feel but total despair at our desperate situation. Caught red-handed, we have no hope for saving either self or country. Our face must register every feeling of our drowning body: our toes, weary beyond belief from trying to elevate that last saving inch; our ankles, chafing at their bonds; our wrists, increasingly raw from attempts to work them loose from the waterlogged fibers of the ropes marrying them together; our shoulders, slumping with the weight of our clothing, which drags us deeper into the void . . ." Holmquist sighed dramatically.

"Perhaps your greater calling was before the camera, Mr. Holmquist," Nelly muttered. "I'd be delighted to give you a turn in *our* tank—"

But the director had, fortunately, already paced off without catching Nelly's remark. Or had he? His attention was now concentrated on a technician. "Can't we go for another inch of water, Bert? If she were actually choking . . ."

"Take that, you filthy saboteur! And that!"

By late afternoon, Fitz was in the midst of an action rescue scene, sparring around the claustrophobic mock-up of a submarine's engine room with Schmidt. He really needn't be spitting out appropriate words. The film was silent, after all, and the dialogue titles to be spliced in during editing would add the necessary comments. But it seemed to put him in the proper mood.

Schmidt was taking his role seriously, too. That last swing at Fitz's face had actually connected, sending Fitz to his knees. Schmidt pursued and the fistfight turned into a wrestling match. Nelly huddled under several blankets, shivering, watching her brother finally get his. Then she began to worry. Why was Schmidt winning? It wasn't written that way in the scenario.

"Cut!" Holmquist strode over to the set and poked at Schmidt's back. "Here, now. Young Dalton's meant to be on top, after all."

Schmidt finally pried himself loose with ill grace and grunted something that might have been an apology.

"All right, Schmidt. That was good stuff and we should be able to use it, but Dalton has to finish the scene by pinning *you*. Is that clear?" Holmquist bent down. "You all right, lad?"

Fitz rose to his feet shaky, but game. "Let me get my hands on that Hun. He nearly broke my jaw!"

"Lovely! I just adore it when my actors truly get into the spirit of things!" Holmquist backed away. "Camera ready? We'll take it from the Hun atop the hero, when the hero, by sheer strength of character, flips the Hun and pins him."

The cameraman began to crank.

Fitz limped on the way home. His face—still shiny from the cold cream used to remove most of the day's greasepaint—was beginning to take on a rather bruised hue. Nelly tipped up her umbrella to better study her brother as they sloshed through rivulets of rainwater drenching the sidewalk.

"What really happened in the engine room this after-noon?"

"I don't know, Sis." His shoulders slumped. "We were fooling around, faking punches. Suddenly Schmidt starts packing power behind it all, growling in German. I guess he just got carried away by the moment. I know I began to do the same thing, thinking about Dad and all." Fitz forgot himself long enough to jump over a large puddle, then stiffened as he was reminded of his aches. "And I may be taller than he, but unfortunately the man's way heavier. All solid-packed muscles, as if he's thrown weights or something."

"What was he saying, Fitz? In German."

"Well, it sounded something like *Deutschland oober all-is,* over and over. I caught the *Deutschland* part, because everybody knows that's the proper name for Germany. Then there were a few *schvines* thrown in . . . I should have elected for German last year in school, instead of French. But popular sentiment was really against it."

"How could I forget? They were calling poor Ben Sal-isbury the 'Beast of Berlin' because he signed up for it. He's nowhere near a German, and he needs the language if he wants to be a scientist."

"You and Ben were kind of sweet on each other, weren't you, Sis."

"Nowhere near as sweet as you were on Katy Cullan!"

"Katy and I? Come on!"

"You carried her books the last two solid weeks of school, Fitz Dalton."

"And what about Ben helping you with your algebra in the school library?"

"You wouldn't help!"

"You never asked me nicely."

Stumbling onto the porch, they carried the argument right upstairs into their kitchen.

"Children! What is going on—" Their mother stopped in dismay, her eyes moving up to her son, then lowering on her daughter. "Fitz, whatever happened to your face? And Nelly, your hair! Straight into a hot tub and shampoo it. Fitz, get my medicine kit. There'd better be good reasons for all of this."

It was a dismal family group that huddled around the kitchen table that night in their bathrobes, spooning down hot soup. The torrents from heaven continued unabated outside the window as Nelly sneezed.

"*Gesundheit.*"

"Well, I guess you do know some German, Fitz, after all."

"Huh?" A dark ring was beginning to form around one of his eyes.

"God bless you, Nelly."

"Thank you, Mother." Nelly swallowed more soup, then looked up. "Have we got any of Daddy's books unpacked yet?"

"I was considering leaving them boxed until the autumn. You know we sold those lovely mahogany bookcases in New York, dear."

"Yes, but couldn't we set a few out on windowsills or something?"

A look of interest entered Fitz's face. "He had some German stuff, didn't he? Maybe even a dictionary . . ."

"I saw a bunch of fruit cases behind the grocery on the way home, Ma. Maybe we could collect them. They'll be wet and dirty, but we could paint them—"

"—and unpack the books," finished Fitz.

Mrs. Dalton stared at her two children uncomprehendingly. Nelly longed to remove the confusion from her mother's face, but she'd privately decided their mother didn't need all the gory details of the day's events. Too much concern over their welfare and they might be hauled out of the motion picture business. She *was* learning a few things never dreamed of by Shakespeare.

"Certainly not tonight. You are both going straight to bed."

Neither of the twins protested.

Holmquist had to send Fitz to the makeup artist for special treatment the next morning. She was working on a melodrama two stages over in the big studio. Nelly trailed after her brother to smirk as he was ordered into a kind of dentist's chair and wrapped in towels.

"Rest your head back, so . . . *Quel extraordinaire* black eye. Ze tones! Such yellow, ze hint of purple sunset . . ." Firm yet delicate fingers traced the hues. "Not to worry, my handsome. Mademoiselle Fifi will fix all."

Mademoiselle Fifi? Nelly choked. The woman was gushing all over poor Fitz. And he was eating it up, even if it was perfectly obvious she was a full-fledged member of the less-well-bred moving-picture caste her mother had been referring to so recently. That low-cut dress, at seven in the morning? Not even a sliver of lace to disguise her prominent attributes. And Fitz's eyes focused directly into their depths. True, with Fifi working on his face that way, there was hardly anywhere else for his eyes to focus. Still, he might try closing them.

"Mother did put some powder on my little brother's bruises not an hour ago—"

"It is so?"

Fifi's head shot up, allowing free range for Fitz's gaze to meet Nelly's. Nelly could clearly read the message in his: "I'll get you for this later!"

"Maybe ze monsoons, they wash it away, yes?"

"Maybe. It does seem to have been raining forever."

"No matter. Zis very special stage pancake, it will cover *tout.*"

Fifi gently massaged a pink base with bluish tones over Fitz's bruises, following it with a heavy dusting with her powder puff. Fitz sneezed. And then a mirror was presented, and towels swept away. "You are new here, *hein*? Come back to Mademoiselle anytime, *mon brave.*"

Fitz almost ran back to their own stage, but Nelly caught up with him. *"Mon brave.* Yuck."

"She was just being pleasant." He halted in mid-stride, next to a musician beating on a tom-tom to give inspiration to the jungle scene being shot beside them. "And since when am I your *little* brother?"

"I was born first. By four and a half minutes. Barely enough time for Dad to get used to having a daughter before rejoicing in a son and heir."

Fitz ran fingers through his thick blond hair. "Listen. If you tell Ma about this, this incident—"

"Careful not to smudge your makeup, little brother." Nelly grinned. "What if?"

"Well, on top of the black eye it wouldn't exactly sound good."

"That some fake Frenchwoman older than Mother was flirting with my brother?"

"She was not older than Mother! Besides, Mother is actually quite young. Without the glasses and dark hair she could almost be taken for *your* twin." The tom-tom was starting to get to him, and Fitz moved on. "And how do you figure Mademoiselle Fifi's a fake?"

Nelly kept pace. "All that pidgin French, for one thing—"

"Daltons!"

The twins, come to another halt and preparing for another verbal round, paused mid-breath. Holmquist was beckoning them through his megaphone.

"Daltons! The tempest is past! The sun shines once more! Onto the garden set for exteriors!"

3
The Fangs of Death

Subduing his Hun opponent by superior fisticuffs, Fitzhugh Dalton obtains the vital information to save his sister, Nelly, from the bowels of the U-boat *Deutschmark* moments before frigid waters engulf her forever. Unfortunately, the water has ruined their hard-won evidence. On consultation, the twins' guardian, Paul Panther, suggests a new ploy: follow—in disguise—the submarine's crew while they are on leave in New York City. Thus the mastermind behind the plans may be discovered.
     —"This Week at the Serials," *Moving Picture World*

Nelly opened the final box of her father's books and began handing them to Fitz. "It's lucky the paint dried on these crates so fast. I was hoping to get at this stuff before another week of shooting at the studio."

"No German dictionary yet?"

"No." She picked up a volume. "But here's the French dictionary I couldn't find last semester." She paged through it. "Let's see what it has to say about *'mon brave.'*"

"Ease off, Nelly, or I might have to mention to Ma all the attentions our screen buddy Lloyd Wright has been lavishing on you."

"He hasn't, either. Just because he brought me a bottle

of Moxie from the studio canteen once or twice—" She stopped. "Wait. Here's the German dictionary finally. Wouldn't you know it, right at the bottom of the last box."

Fitz snatched at it and began flipping pages. "*S . . . sch . . .* no *schv*'s. Must be a 'w.' They use a lot of them." He scanned a column. "Here it is. *Sch*-w-*ein.* Apparently the 'w' is pronounced hard, like a 'v.' " The definition finally registered. "That *schwein*!"

"What does it mean?" Nelly pulled the book away. " 'Pig'! It means 'pig'! We should have been able to figure out that one all by ourselves."

"I don't think I care much for our Mr. Schmidt. Let me have another go at that book, Nell."

She relinquished it. "What are you hunting for now?"

"Just wanted to see if it could cast any light on 'cigars' or 'dumplings'." Fitz finally shut the dictionary and added it to the new shelves. "Nope. What do you suppose Dad was going on about in that note Ma remembered, Nelly?"

"Maybe it was just a shopping list. Maybe he wanted to bring some guests home for dinner—"

"And the menu for Mother was eggs and dumplings? I don't think so, Sis." Fitz slowly unwrapped his legs from his position on the floor and got up to stretch. "I need to walk off some of this frustration. The pawnshop should still be open. Now that our budget can handle it, how about we get Ma's typewriter out of hock?"

The twins took turns carrying the heavy Remington. When they paused several blocks from home by the door of the local library, Fitz set the machine down. "Whew. I'm glad we won't have to be lugging this back for a good long time—never, let's hope." He sat on a step next to it. "Did you notice all that stuff at the pawnbroker's, Nell? Guitars and guns and jewelry . . ."

"Abandoned dreams, Fitz." Nelly settled herself next to a granite statue of a small sleeping lion. She stroked its mane contemplatively. "It was sad. I'll be relieved when we can buy back Ma's ruby earrings. Maybe next month, in time for her birthday . . ."

Fitz didn't seem to be listening. "Guns. There was even a German pistol. It made me think about Schmidt again."

"What about Schmidt?"

"Well, you know how Ma's written this coming week's scenario? About how we're supposed to follow the Germans around to try to find their New York base?"

"Yes?" Nelly wasn't sure she cared for what she suspected her brother was on the verge of suggesting.

"What if . . . what if such a place actually existed? And if it did, how would one find such a hotbed of Germans?" He answered his own question triumphantly. "We follow a genuine German! And since Schmidt is the only genuine German we know . . . What if we were to follow him after work on Monday?"

Nelly's hand shot off the stone lion. It definitely appeared to have leered wickedly at her. "I don't like it. In the first place, we don't know that Schmidt's anything but what he pretends to be."

"A bad-tempered German-American who needs work enough to hang around the studio waiting for bit parts?"

"Exactly. He might have a wife at home, and a batch of little children."

"With his disposition, and that scar?"

"Some women might find that scar attractive."

"Do you?"

Nelly shivered.

"Enough said." Fitz got up and leaned over the type-writer. "Just think about it, that's all. I don't like the way he was laying into me the other day, for no good reason. And the way he skulks around us at the studio, sort of listening." He paused before picking up the Remington. "Come to think of it, his build is mighty close to that of our own mysterious eavesdropper, sort of chunky and hulking . . ."

"That's silly, Fitz. And unfair to Schmidt. Holmquist didn't even hire him till the following morning—"

"I'm the one who chased the blackguard last week, remember? Anyhow, mum's the word to Ma. She doesn't need any more worries."

"Do you take me for an idiot?"

"Hush. No insults intended." He hoisted the machine, then paused to examine the building before them specu-latively. "Do you suppose . . ."

"The library closes in half an hour, Fitz, and we've already found Dad's dictionaries. And enough old novels to keep both of us busy—if we ever found a spare moment to read them."

The typewriter was lowered onto the library step once more. "Not that, Sis. I've been considering Black Tom again. We never even saw the newspapers when they came out—"

"Even *The New York Times* couldn't bring Dad back again. You remember how Ma had to hide us from reporters for what seemed like days after. They were absolute vultures—"

"—pecking at what was left of the carcass. Us," her brother finished. "Still, there might be a few clues in the articles." He stopped to stare at his sister. "Are you game to try?"

Nelly shrugged and leaned against the recumbent lion, then backed off, just in case. "I think that was one reason Ma didn't really mind leaving New York for the summer. With the War on, and spy stories coming out in the papers again . . . not to mention that reporter who tracked us down last month wanting to reopen the old wounds—"

Fitz snickered. "You were hilarious, Sis. There was Ma, politely standing him off at the apartment door—"

"Well, he wouldn't go away, would he? Mother is just too civilized sometimes. Even after he insulted her by offering money for an exclusive interview!"

Fitz kicked at the waiting typewriter, then remembered it was his mother's lifeline. "Newspaper writers! No sense of ethics, the lot of them. As if we'd accept money from Dad's death!"

"Exactly. And there you were, hovering with your tongue in your mouth. What other choice had I but to muss my hair and wander down the hallway doing Ophelia's mad scene from *Hamlet?* I had to practice it for my English class the next day anyway. That scared him off."

Fitz shook his head. "Maybe you always had more of a dramatic bent than I suspected." He stooped to retrieve the typewriter. "Open the door, will you? A library's bound to have back issues."

The twins stared at the bold headlines: MUNITIONS EXPLOSIONS SHAKE NEW YORK; WRECK $7,000,000 JERSEY STORAGE PLANT; MANY KILLED; ALARM AND DAMAGE HERE.

"Sunday, July 30, 1916," Fitz murmured. "The day of infamy for the Dalton Family."

" 'Bridges Tremble; City Is Terror-Stricken,' " Nelly read aloud. " 'Police Called to Prevent Looting of Stores.' Goodness, it was a mess, wasn't it? All I remember is Mother dragging us out of the house in the middle of the night with the servants when she thought we'd been hit by an earthquake."

"And returning home to our beds to find the police waiting. They weren't much more sympathetic than the reporters."

Nelly was flipping through the stack of old papers to the next issue. "They certainly weren't. Look at Monday. The losses are up to twenty million and they've begun arresting Black Tom Island's owners for negligence. I suppose they would've arrested Dad, too, if he hadn't saved them the trouble."

"Maybe this was a bad idea, Nell. Shall I put the papers away?"

"No." Nelly was poring over the articles. "The victims aren't even buried yet, and all the Manhattan merchants are worried about is whether their insurance companies will pay for a million dollars' worth of broken plate glass."

Fitz wasn't listening. His eye had caught another column. "Take a gander at this! It's a list of accidents at explosives factories since the War started in Europe in 1914."

Nelly redirected her attention to the column. "Gracious. It's a very long list. They couldn't all have been accidents, could they?"

"In a pig's eye!"

The twins were distracted by a discreetly cleared throat. The librarian loomed over them, celluloid collar loosened at the neck, tie limp in the heat. "Excuse me?"

"Yes, sir?"

"Try not to crumple those papers. They seem to have been in demand recently. And the library is about to close."

"Yes, sir. We'll be careful. We're almost finished, anyway." Fitz paged madly through the next several days' issues. "Tuesday: 'Insurance Men Busy Calculating Losses; City Cleans Debris.' Wednesday: an Editorial.

"Had Sunday morning's explosion over in Jersey City taken place a year or so ago, when there was some reason for believing, and more for suspecting, resort by persons in this country to criminal devices for the purpose of stopping the flow of American-made munitions to the Allies, there would have been a widespread tendency to ascribe the disaster to the plotters who were then accused of doing much work of the same sort. Now that theory receives little attention . . . From all that is known or seems likely ever to be known, its origin was in one or another form of the carelessness to which at least nine out of ten of our fires are due . . ."

"I'm locking the doors, you kids!"

"Coming!" Fitz rapidly scanned headlines for another few days. "That's it, Sis." He got up, clutching the Remington. "Not even a seven-day wonder. Black Tom and Dad were written off in under a week."

"Carelessness, my foot!" Nelly fumed as the library doors slammed shut behind them. "What about Dad's list? What about the story he promised Mother?"

"Patience, Sis." Fitz huffed over the machine. "Patience. And I think it's your turn to carry this monster."

Monday afternoon, Holmquist was rummaging through a trunk filled with disguises. "Ah. The very thing for you, young Dalton." His hand came out flourishing a furry, caterpillar-like object.

"Ugh." Nelly pulled away. "Are you sure it isn't alive?"

The director chuckled. "Not yet. We merely add a dab of glue . . . Mr. Dalton, present face!"

Fitz stood still while the indignity was perpetrated upon him. In a moment he sported an impressive black mustache, its ends long enough for twirling. Fitz stroked the appendage as he turned to Nelly. "I say, old girl, have you a spot of mustache wax on you?"

"It matches your blond hair beautifully, Fitz."

Holmquist was also studying the effect, hand on chin. "The hair. Of course." He dove back into the trunk. "Easily fixed." This time he emerged with a black wig, which he tossed at Fitz. "Try that on for size."

Askew, the mop transformed Fitz into a distinctly

seedy individual. Nelly giggled, then stopped herself. It was her turn next.

Holmquist was considering. "A *femme fatale,* I think."

Shortly Nelly was swathed in a long brocade wrap, trimmed in moth-eaten fur. A huge ostrich-feathered hat hid all of her face not covered by a thick, dark veil. Nelly squinted through the grid lines and blew at the veil. It tickled. She certainly hoped fashions changed before she'd have to wear such a monstrosity in real life.

"Excellent! The transformations will be enough to amuse our audience, without confusing them." He picked up his megaphone. "Camera, outside. We'll do establishing shots this afternoon, then motor into the city in the morning for a few location scenes. Lloyd, we'll need you to admire Miss Dalton's disguise." Hiking up his jodhpurs, Holmquist strode forth.

The cameraman shook his bald head and began to dolly out the camera.

"Need a hand, Sam?" Fitz asked.

"Thanks, Fitz. Our bloody director has delusions of grandeur, in case you haven't noticed. Running all of us ragged, overtime every day. Wants to make out to the producers that his talents are wasted on mere serials."

Fitz pushed against the machine with good will. "What's he after, then, Sam?"

"Hollywood, California, is what. Since Mr. Griffith's gone out to the orange groves and permanent sunshine, Holmquist figures that's where the future of the industry lies."

"Is it true?"

The cameraman nodded. "Probably. A couple of the smaller studios are already packing up. I suppose I will, too, after a while. If I want work. But I don't even like oranges."

The sky was becoming dark too early when the twins were excused for the day. Nelly inspected it.

"We'd better hurry home, Fitz. There's a storm brewing."

"All the better for our nefarious schemes, my dear," he rasped with appropriately dramatic menace.

"Fitz, you aren't still serious about following Schmidt? Are you?"

"Halt for the transformation!" Fitz dug into his knickers and pulled out a scrofulous object.

"Eek!" Nelly jumped away. "A dead rat!"

"Nonsense. Merely a deceased beard from Holmquist's trunk. It's a little sticky, though. Give me a hand, Nell."

"You really mean to do this, don't you. You want to hound that poor man only because he has the misfortune of having the wrong background in a time of war. Our country is supposed to be a melting pot, after all. He should be given the benefit of a doubt—"

"Listen, Sis. Save the civics lecture. You don't want to help, you can go on home to Ma. I'll shadow Schmidt myself."

Nelly picked up an end of the beard with two fingers and began attaching it to her brother's face. "We'll do it together, or not at all. Although after studying those old papers this weekend and recalling just what a prob-

lem the press was . . ." She poked at the beard dili-
gently.

"Ouch! A little less enthusiasm, please. It's not meant
to stick for life."

"Remember what the librarian said about someone else
reading those *Times* articles? Reporters do a lot of background research like that. The papers have been packed
with remotely related war stories. How do we know the
snooper outside our kitchen window wasn't a reporter trying for a free scoop?"

"We don't. Neither do we know it was Schmidt. Consider this an exploratory foray. Just to see if he does anything suspicious. We don't exactly have hordes of other
suspects at hand . . . Do watch where you're fastening the
beard, Sis. That ridiculous greasepaint is making my face
break out."

"You're not the only one," Nelly commiserated.
"Thank heavens Holmquist lets us apply and remove it
at the studio. My reputation could be ruined for life just
walking home in that stuff." She stood back to inspect
her handiwork. "Well, I guess the shadowing couldn't
hurt if we consider it to be practice. We've got to start
somewhere. Where is Schmidt, anyway?"

"Last I saw, he was talking with Paul Panther." Fitz
felt his furry face. Apparently satisfied, he dug in his
other pocket. "Here, Nelly, for you."

"What is it?" She slowly unwound the object, revealing
a much mangled cloche hat and a pair of glassless spectacles.

"Put 'em on. They'll do wonders."

"Don't you ever stop to think who wore these things before, Fitz? I mean, they could have fleas, or lice, or—"

"Enough." He shoved her against a wall of the studio. "Here comes Schmidt now. In a hurry."

An ominous rumble of thunder shook the evening sky.

Schmidt never once looked back. The twins followed him at a decent distance, darting behind trees and the occasional delivery wagon. Their stealth appeared unnecessary as he barreled ahead, single-minded, through the lowering storm. It was after only three blocks of pursuit that Fitz stopped.

Nell puffed next to him. "What is it? Why are you stopping?"

"Have you noticed the direction he's taking?"

Nelly peered through her veil, blinking slowly as recognition registered. "Why, this is the way we go home every day. In fact, our house is just past the park in the next street!" She began to move.

"Wait. Let's watch what he does." Fitz held her back as a massive clap of thunder crashed above them. Farther down the street a bolt of lightning struck at the edges of their little park, right next to Schmidt. He broke into a run as the rain beat down.

Nelly ripped off her black veil. "This is ridiculous, Fitz. Even Schmidt is running." The green satin of the cloche hat began to sag, its dye oozing down Nelly's neck.

Fitz loped off. "Yes, but the question is, where?"

Past the park, Schmidt had mysteriously vanished. Fitz paused to tug at his beard. "Nuts! We lost him."

The rain was coming down in sheets, and Nelly didn't even bother to respond. She leaped for the steps of their house and the safety of its porch. Fitz was not far behind.

Dripping and heaving, Nelly glared at her brother. "What next, mastermind?"

"A hot supper, I hope."

Several days of shooting around the streets of New York passed. After the company of actors was deposited back at the studio each evening, Fitz and Nelly doggedly continued their pursuit of Schmidt. He took the same route each day. On the second evening they discovered why.

"I told you so!" Nelly proclaimed in a superior tone.

Fitz stared at Schmidt, disappearing into a boarding-house two blocks beyond their own. "So he was only heading home, after all." He shrugged in defeat. "It was worth a try."

Nothing further was said about pursuing Schmidt or taking any other course of action. By Friday, Nelly was relieved to have that one less worry. This was the day, after all, on which she was scheduled to meet the Fangs of Death.

The Fangs of Death. Nelly shuddered each time she thought of her forthcoming ordeal. It was only three weeks into the shooting of the serial, and already her mother's overactive imagination held Nelly in dread. Who would have thought such an otherwise sweet, sensible parent could dredge such horrors out of her mind for her only daughter? Who would have thought such a caring mother could leave the beast in question—or worse yet, beasts—unspecified? Open to any interpretation whatsoever by Cedric Holmquist?

"Stop dawdling so, Nell, we'll be late for work."

Nelly felt for her security-badge brooch, patted it absently, and walked even more slowly. "Easy for you to say, Fitz. You don't have to deal with the Horrors of Hell today."

"How do you figure that? I'm the one who has to keep the Fangs of Death from ripping out your throat."

"Hah! It's far easier to be the defender than the rippee."

"That remains to be seen. Shake a leg."

Reluctantly, Nelly improved her pace.

"Two minutes late, Daltons." Cedric Holmquist was in leather pants and jacket today, complete with short whip. He looked, in fact, rather as if he were about to take on a troupe of circus lions. Nelly hoped she was not meant to be the centerpiece of the ring.

"Oh, this is going to be a fun scene." He glanced briefly at the script in his free hand. "The Hunmaster—discovered, but not unmasked—has encountered our Nelly closing in on his lair. Choosing not to bloody his own hands, he unleashes his secret weapon upon the fair damsel and departs, confident in the knowledge that his ravenous beast will do his bidding, as usual."

So it was to be interpreted as one beast only. Nelly sighed with relief while Holmquist smiled with anticipated pleasure.

"Makeup applied? Slip into your *femme fatale* wrap, please, Miss Dalton . . . Good. Now cower suggestively in that dark nook we have prepared for you. Lights? Camera?"

"One moment, please, Mr. Holmquist . . ."

"Yes, Miss Dalton?"

"About the Fangs of Death?"

"Time is money, Miss Dalton. Spit it out."

"Would it be possible . . ." She gulped. "Would it be possible to meet prior to the shooting? That is, the Fangs and I. It might make my reaction more appropriate."

Holmquist paused. "Well, I was hoping for it to be a surprise. I *like* surprises."

"I don't, Mr. Holmquist."

The director considered. "Still . . . I suppose it couldn't hurt the dramatic intensity of the moment that much." He brightened. "You have been developing your hysteria levels nicely. Henry!"

An underling poked his head around the set. "Yes, Mr. Holmquist?"

"Bring on Fangs, if you please."

Nelly held her breath. She knew the studio kept a small zoo on the premises. Could it be a cougar, perhaps? An undersized cougar she could handle. She might even be able to manage an elderly lion . . .

A huge, joyous bark broke her concentration. Before she could exhale, a vast furry body dashed into sight and sprang at her, paws foremost. Nelly's breath was driven out of her by the crash of those paws against her chest. Hot breath and a very moist tongue slid all over her face.

"No, Fangs. No!" Henry the keeper had caught up with his charge. "Heel, Fangs! Good dog. Now sit!"

Fangs heeled and sat, his tail thumping a mile a minute as he kept Nelly in his sights. Nelly laughed at the grinning dog. He was the biggest German Shepherd she'd ever seen. And he was as dangerous as a pussycat.

"Never seen Fangs take to anybody like he just took to you, miss," Henry the keeper allowed. "Usually a mite tough to handle, he is. But it seems like he sniffed you right from his cage." He patted the animal's head thoughtfully. "Some do say that great beasts like this only have one soul mate, and keep on searching for that one their entire lives."

Fangs thumped and gave one short bark of agreement. Holmquist scratched his head with his whip hand, bringing the weapon unconsciously closer to Nelly. Fangs growled. The director jumped and dropped the whip.

"I knew it should have remained a surprise!"

Holmquist was correct. Fangs adamantly refused to approach Nelly with anything bordering on hostility. On successive orders from his trainer, he finally turned, hackles raised, on Henry himself. Henry backed off.

"With your permission, Mr. Holmquist"—the trainer finally gave in to defeat—"I think this is going to have to be a job for Tessie."

Holmquist waved his arms. "Just get rid of that dog. He's wasted enough of our time. And bring on Tessie at once," he added.

Nellie relaxed as Fangs was led docilely away. Anything named Tessie she could deal with. She tightened her brocade wrap, mussed her loose hair becomingly, and cowered back into her corner. It was Fitz's gasp that led her to raise her eyes. They opened wider, and wider, and from her throat a scream eased forth, growing with heart-stopping intensity.

Tessie was a Bengal tiger.

"I think you finally graduated into the ranks of acting professionals today, Sis. At least in our director's eyes." Fitz chivalrously held the studio door for his sister. She wafted through, shoulders straight, head high, still spitting mad.

"Regarding *our director:* Lucky for him Tessie was declawed, toothless, and practically senile. If that maniac Holmquist ever pulls another surprise like that on me, he'll be graduating himself—to directing choirs of angels."

"Sure you've got the right location in mind for our noble director, Nell?"

Nelly glanced at her brother, then finally laughed. Fitz joined her, and in another moment they were both in convulsions. The hilarity stopped only when a harsh growl distracted them. Fitz cast around for the origin of the sound.

"For pete's sake, Nell. Right behind you—in a protective stance. It's your secret admirer."

"Fangs!" She knelt to embrace the dog. "How did you get out of your cage? How did you get away from Henry?"

The studio door swung open behind them, and a very harried Henry raced out. "Have you got him? Thank heavens!" He had a leash in hand and was already approaching the dog. "Come now, Fangs. It was naughty of you to escape that way."

Fangs bared his teeth.

"Never seen anything like it. A madman he was, all the afternoon. Finally chewed through the very wire of his cage, he did, and sprinted off."

Nelly took the dog's muzzle in her hand and gently examined it. "Poor thing. You've given yourself a few cuts, haven't you."

Fangs whimpered meekly.

Henry crept up. Just as he was about to fasten the leash on the German Shepherd's collar, Fangs snapped. "Ow! Bad dog!" Henry backed off with alacrity. "Never touched me before. Wasn't always easy to get along with, but he never harmed me." Henry was obviously bewildered.

"Would you like me to lead him back for you, Henry?"

"Would you, miss?"

"Certainly. Heel, Fangs."

Fangs obediently followed Nelly, tail waving, as far as the studio door. Nelly opened the door. "Come, Fangs."

Fangs stopped. Nelly patted him, then called again. The dog obstinately refused to reenter the studio. Nelly stared first at Fitz, next at Henry. "What shall I do?"

Henry was nursing his hand. "Take the brute home for the weekend. That's obviously what he wants. He's not scheduled for shooting anyhow."

Nelly hesitated. She'd never owned a pet before. Not since that last Christmas present from barely remembered grandparents when she was five. It was a tremendously charming kitten, but her father had proven allergic to it. "What does he eat?"

"Anything. And lots of it." Henry handed her the leash

and full responsibility. Then he escaped back into the studio.

Fitz eyed his sister. "What's Mother going to say?"

Dorothy Dalton reluctantly tore her eyes from the typewriter as her children stuck their heads in the apartment door.

"Dinner's going to be a little late, I'm afraid. I got caught up in another scene—" She never finished, because Fangs had shoved through the door and leaped upon her, nearly knocking her from her perch on a kitchen chair. Long tongue bathed nose and glasses ecstatically. "What in the world!"

Fitz dryly made the introductions. "Meet Fangs, Ma. It seems he's a dog without peer. In one day he's found two soul mates."

4
Catacombs of Calamity

Saved from a ravenous Bengal tiger by her valiant twin
brother, Nelly Dalton is being attended by doctors in her
luxurious bedroom. Against their recommendations, she
struggles forth from her sickbed to wreak vengeance on the
masked mastermind of the Kaiser's secret war against
America. Still-unknown traps await her . . .
—"This Week at the Serials," *Moving Picture World*

"You're doing it again, Mother!"

Mrs. Dalton was examining soup bones recently
fetched from the butcher. "Doing what, Nelly dear? And
do you think Fangs would like to gnaw on this thigh-
bone? It has a little meat—"

Fangs answered for himself by lunging for the bone.
As his jaws clasped fast, he eased it, surprisingly gently,
from his patroness's grip, to settle blissfully at her feet.

"This animal is going to eat us out of house and home."
Dorothy Dalton smiled dotingly on the beast in question
while a growl emerged from Fitz.

"Truer words were never spoken. He's been here
twenty-four hours and there's nothing left for *me* to eat."

He made a face at his mother's pile of bones. "Nothing not *raw.*"

"Why, Brother, I do believe you're jealous of Fangs. Just because he doesn't seem to take to you—"

As if following the conversation, Fangs heaved himself from the floor and, bone in mouth, padded over to Fitz, seated on the kitchen windowsill. The dog paused expectantly, then pressed the bone on Fitz.

"My word, children, Fangs wants to make friends."

Fitz, still in awe of the animal, tentatively reached for the offering. "It's all slimy!" He shoved it back. Fangs nodded and retreated under the kitchen table with his booty.

"I'd call that an armed truce, wouldn't you, Mother?"

"Indeed I would, Nell." She laughed and threw the remaining bones into a pot of water. "If only America and Germany could come as close in their peace negotiations." The pot was placed on the stove. "What did you start off saying, Nelly?"

"Oh." Nelly patted the scenario for Episode Four of *In the Kaiser's Clutch,* which lay before her on the table. "Fitz is still getting all the superlatives. 'Valiant,' 'heroic'—it turns my stomach!"

Fitz growled again, and Fangs could be heard dropping his bone to yelp questioningly.

"Simmer down, Fangs," Fitz directed at the dog. "No enemies in sight." He turned to his sister. "Why can't I be valiant and heroic? My exploits are just as hair-raising as yours. This coming week alone, I'm to negotiate a subterranean chamber fairly clanking with dried bones—"

Fangs thumped his tail approvingly.

"Lay off the kibitzing, Fangs." Fitz frowned. "Where was I? Oh, yes. Negotiating subterranean chambers—"

"Oozing with mold and fungus and other nasties, all of which *I* have to negotiate first," finished Nelly.

"Children," their mother diplomatically interrupted, "I believe it's time to walk the dog."

"Again?" fumed Fitz.

"He's a large dog. He needs a lot of exercise."

Outside, Fangs nearly pulled Nelly's arm out of its socket as he lunged on his leash for a squirrel. Nelly relinquished the leash. "I don't think he's getting enough to eat, Fitz," she worried.

"I don't think there'll ever be enough for him to eat, Nell." He watched as the dog treed the squirrel. "What are we going to do with him?"

"I suppose the studio will want him back—"

"He won't go. That's perfectly obvious."

"Then we'll just have to keep him, won't we." Nelly smiled.

"Abducted him, that's what you've gone and done." Henry the animal keeper's attitude had changed from relief to truculence by Monday morning, undoubtedly because the studio held him accountable for Fangs. "Where is the brute, anyway?"

"He's home, looking after our mother," Nelly answered. "Strange, but it's as if he knew we were coming to the studio. He absolutely refused to join us."

Henry washed his hands metaphorically. "You'll have

to beard the Business Office, then, not me. There'll be restitution to pay. A valuable animal, he was."

"Not that valuable, if you couldn't control him—"

Holmquist was bustling over. "Still nattering about that creature, are we?" He shivered delicately. "Pathmark is well rid of him. An absolute danger to life and limb. Why, he could even be rabid—"

"Never!" yelped Nelly.

"Tut, tut. I was merely using exaggeration to make a point. Do come along, Miss Dalton. We've got the trapdoor functioning, and we have to practice your graceful tumble through it."

Nelly did not tumble gracefully through the trapdoor. After three tries she was ruefully wiping at fresh scrapes along one cheek. Holmquist examined her face.

"That won't do. Not at all. We'll have to pad the edges of the hole. In the meantime, I'm afraid it's off to Mademoiselle Fifi for you, Miss Dalton. Our audience enjoys high adventure, but they'd prefer it to remain bloodless."

Grumbling, Nelly set off through the studio in search of the resident makeup artist. Fifi was discovered cooing over Paul Panther as she added artistically dark smudges under his eyes. The latest scenario had begun to suggest that the twins' guardian might possibly have been visiting in Central Europe during his recent mysterious travels. That put a whole different complexion on the man's motivations.

"*Restez tranquille.* Soon I shall have you looking like ze Dark Invader himself, *mon brave*—"

Panther jerked convulsively in his seat, then settled down again. "Sorry, Fifi. Your brush caught my eye."

Unseen in the background, Nelly watched. Had the brush gone near his eye? Or had the *"mon brave"* endearment set him fidgeting so? Nelly grinned to herself. Fifi seemed to use that term indiscriminately on any male, even the fortyish, hook-nosed Panther . . . And that "Dark Invader" comment—what a curious name for Mademoiselle to come up with. Then again, she did know the serial plot was anti-German . . . Probably just her eccentric flair for words. It surely wasn't in any of Mother's current scripts, although it wasn't a bad term for the master villain. Nelly considered further. Not bad at all. She'd have to mention it over dinner.

Towels were swept off, and Panther sprang up to grasp Mademoiselle Fifi's hand. With a small bow, he raised it briefly to his lips, then strode off, whistling.

"Such a rascal, that one." Fifi admired her hand for a moment. "He so likes to play ze Continental role. I become more than makeup artist for *tout le studio* . . ." Fifi turned with a smile to acknowledge Nelly. "Another customer. Ze big sister herself!"

Suddenly Nelly laughed. Maybe the woman wasn't so bad at that. Maybe her pidgin French wasn't even fake. "Director Holmquist wants my cheeks spotless, mademoiselle."

"*Pauvre chérie,* then he should protect you from ze accidents, *n'est-ce pas?* Sit. I fix. Even ze alcohol first, so there should be no infections, *oui?*"

Nelly sank into the chair. "Thank you, mademoiselle."

Fitz was not enthusiastic, but he did accompany his sister to the Business Office of Pathmark Studios during their luncheon period. It was in a sort of glassed-in tower that rose several stories above the massive studio itself, no doubt to allow management to oversee all operations.

The office staff was incredulous at their request, and the twins were shunted from secretary to secretary until they found themselves in the presence of the studio manager himself.

Enoch Morris, fat, bald, and chomping on an unlit cigar, listened to their story with one raised eyebrow.

"Sure you're not in league with the enemy? Behind some of these threatening anonymous notes we've been getting? Three weeks with Pathmark and you've managed to sabotage my zoo!"

"Threatening notes? No, sir, not at all. Fangs just refused to come back—"

Morris managed a half-grin around his cigar butt. "The keeper did report to me—a little more defensively than necessary, under the circumstances."

Nelly's face lit up. "Then it will be all right for us to keep Fangs?"

"I'll have his cost deducted from your pay this week."

Fitz became suspicious. "How much, Mr. Morris?"

"It must be taken under advisement. Fangs did break his contract, after all." The audience completed, Morris waved them out.

"There go Ma's ruby earrings." Fitz was glum all the way down the steps of the office tower. "And what was that stuff about threatening notes?"

Nelly was more concerned about Fangs. "Mr. Morris

couldn't really charge more than ten or fifteen dollars, could he?"

"I'm not sure, Sis, but we'll find out soon enough. I just hope your mutt is worth the price."

Holmquist was pacing around the tunnel set, fuming. "Has anyone seen Schmidt? He was supposed to play the masked mastermind this afternoon!"

Paul Panther answered from the pile of skeletons he was lounging against. "I think he left right after checking in this morning, Cedric. He was complaining about a migraine—"

"Who ever heard of a German with a migraine? Germans are supposed to be invincible to bodily pain!"

Panther shrugged. "He'll probably be fine by tomorrow. He ought to be. He hit me up for a few bucks for aspirin money till payday." A rueful grin followed. "The last time was for beer money. I guess that's what comes of going out of your way to make the extras feel comfortable . . . We could always do the bedroom scenes this afternoon."

Holmquist stopped his pacing to glare at a set designer. "Did you find those satin pillows, Earl? At least six of them? Good." He focused on Nelly. "It seems you'll have a respite from your travails after all, Miss Dalton. Wrap a scarf artfully around your neck. You have tiger claw marks to disguise."

Mrs. Dalton was studying the evening paper, Fangs's head lodged on her feet, when the twins got home. "There's been another munitions plant accident."

"Where, Mother?" Nelly bent to greet the dog.

"Jersey City. Not nearly as bad as Black Tom, of course, or we would have seen the smoke. Still, it is a setback to the war effort."

"Was it sabotage, Ma?" Fitz was already attacking a loaf of bread.

"It's suspected. Some kind of a mysterious detonating device. Thank heavens no one was injured. Just an estimated $20,000 damage."

"Phew," Fitz whistled. "*Just.* Not that it holds a candle to Black Tom's millions—"

"How would you know about that, Fitz?"

"Well, Ma . . . Oh, Nelly and I were reading some of the old papers the other day."

"I thought we weren't going to return to all that, Fitzhugh. I thought we were trying to move forward."

"You're the one who remembered Dad's list, Ma. Sometimes you have to go backwards a little to move forward."

Mrs. Dalton smiled gently at her son. "You are growing up, in more ways than one."

Fitz grinned, only to return to his younger self. "Anyway, I'd love to get my hands on those son of a guns. Only for a minute. I'd give them what for. I'd pummel 'em clear to China!" Fitz pantomimed a mean right hook, followed by a left that could have removed Schmidt's face. Fangs raised himself on his haunches and growled, putting an end to the demonstration.

Nelly laughed and hugged the dog. "What a pitiful Teuton you are, boy. You truly can't stand violence, can you?"

Fangs licked her face.

"I must say that dog is a comfort," Mrs. Dalton commented. "I don't feel so alone anymore writing by myself. Not so afraid of unwelcome callers . . ."

"There haven't been any more reporters around, have there, Mother?"

"Don't be silly, Nelly. How could they have tracked us from Manhattan? I expressly neglected to leave a forwarding address . . ." Mrs. Dalton stopped at the looks on her children's faces. "Who needs to find us, anyway? We've no immediate relatives, and our fair-weather friends disappeared with the house, the servants, and the furniture. Your school chums will see you in the fall."

"What about your manuscripts, Mother?" Nelly asked. "You've quite a few articles waiting at magazines—"

"*They* received change-of-address notes." Mrs. Dalton returned to a lighter subject. "Fangs even helped me through a few writer's blocks today, when I just didn't know what to make up next."

Fitz, pulling bowls down from a shelf, played along with his mother's game. "You've been talking to him, Ma?"

"And why not, may I ask? He's almost as good as someone my own age to talk to. And his demands are certainly simpler." She folded the paper. "So what happened to you two today?"

Nelly launched into a description of their interview with Enoch Morris, then moved on to Mademoiselle Fifi and the Dark Invader business while Fitz ladled soup into the bowls.

"Goodness, but Mr. Panther kisses hands elegantly.

And don't you think 'Dark Invader' is a terrific name, Mother?" Nelly picked up her spoon. "You made dumplings! Huge ones!"

"Just trying to stretch the soup, dear."

Fitz stared at his own bowl. Then, unaccountably, he stuck his fingers into it and fished out a dumpling.

"Fitz, what in the world!"

It was hotter than he'd expected, and Fitz yelped and tossed the lump into the air. It came down off course, right into Fangs's waiting mouth. With a gulp, it was gone.

"Fitz Dalton, you'd better have a very good reason—"

But Fitz was still considering the invisible arc of the dumpling. "Only a little bigger, and it could be a grenade," he muttered.

"You'd better stop insulting Ma's food, Fitz. You didn't even taste it first."

"Can't you see I'm thinking, Sis?" His spoon tapped the table in an insistent beat until a smile stretched across his face. "Dad's shopping list. Is it possible it was in some sort of code?"

Nelly began to catch on. "You mean 'dumplings' could mean a type of grenade? . . . What would that make 'cigars'?"

"I'm not certain. Maybe a different kind of bomb, disguised."

"Perhaps you should be writing my next serial installment, Fitz," Dorothy Dalton commented. "If you think my scenarios are farfetched . . ."

Fitz got up to snare another dumpling from the pot. "Stranger things have been known to happen, Mother.

Aren't munitions workers being searched at factory gates? A really good sabotage device would have to be disguised as something else. Like a cigar, or a pencil . . . or maybe even a *dumpling* in a lunch pail."

Mrs. Dalton shook her head. "It is really impossible to escape the past, isn't it?"

True to Panther's prediction, Schmidt appeared on the set bright and early the next morning. Nelly studied him covertly. He certainly didn't look like anyone who would ever have a migraine. There was nothing in the least bit sensitive or delicate about the man . . . His wiry hair was cropped shorter than ever this morning, though, with just the hint of a dun-colored singe around one temple.

Fitz poked her. "Stop staring, Nell. Schmidt's beginning to notice."

She turned away, whispering in her brother's ear, "Take a look at the haircut. The right side, especially."

"Later. Holmquist wants to do the tunnel scene now."

Fitz was beginning to understand Sam the cameraman's earlier comments about their director—especially the part about Holmquist's trying to rise above the serial genre. Most serials Fitz'd seen had at least one episode revolving around a dark tunnel. It was expected, and his mother had naturally included one. Holmquist had taken that standard scene and was currently trying to raise it to *Art.*

Fitz stood on a scaffold next to Sam. The camera was pointing down into a veritable labyrinth of passageways that Holmquist had had constructed. Nelly was meant to run through this maze with increasing frenzy.

"Just like a trapped rat," Fitz thought aloud.

"Fairly clever, at that," Sam commented placidly. "But it does require a second camera. I hope we'll be able to catch it all."

Nelly began her run, and the cameras cranked. Halfway through, she seemed to become disoriented. Holmquist, next to the second cameraman atop another tower of scaffolding on the far side of the maze, yelled encouragement through his megaphone. "Excellent, Miss Dalton. The walls are closing in on you. Was it the right turn you wanted, or the left?"

Nelly chose the left and ran again, panting audibly through the open ceilings of the labyrinth.

"Claustrophobia is becoming a real, visceral thing, Miss Dalton! Your hair is coming undone, you need to clasp your heart . . . Who *knows* what might be around the next turn? Ernest! Where are those giant cockroaches!"

Nelly ground to a halt next to a leering skull embedded in the wall whose eye sockets glowed, beady and bright. Silly. Empty sockets didn't have eyes . . . But these did, and they moved. Six-inch insects began crawling forth, one after the other.

"Eeeek!"

"Well done, Miss Dalton, yet that is but the beginning. We must run, run, run for our very life, not knowing—but suspecting—something far worse to come!"

The something far worse was Schmidt, hooded evil

incarnate, lurking at the end of the last corridor. Nelly
raced right into him, to jump back, totally aquiver.

"Fantastic! Cut! We'll do the close-ups later. Mr. Dalton? Mr. Dalton, what are you doing on that camera plat-
form? Down, down. It's your turn to pursue!"

Holmquist fussed with the tunnel scenes for the rest of
the week. He seemed fascinated by his own cleverness and
had scores of atmosphere shots exposed: the giant cockroaches munching on carrion; close-ups of rats with their
pointy teeth aglow (he'd had them, as well as the fake
skeletons and bone piles, painted in phosphorescent
hues); slimy ooze, inching down dark corridors. On Friday morning he had a final brainstorm and called for
Henry the zookeeper.

Henry arrived worried. "The cockroaches haven't died,
have they? I had to borrow them from the Bronx Zoo.
They're quite rare—from some part of German East
Africa, or was it Togoland? But with the War on . . ."

"The cockroaches, I assure you, are ecstatically happy,
Henry. They're particularly fond of steak tartare."

Henry blanched. "The Bronx people did say not to feed
them anything really *fresh*. Something about triggering a
cannibalistic mechanism—"

"Tut, tut. It's not cockroaches we're here to discuss,
Henry. It's frogs."

"Frogs?"

"Frogs or toads." Holmquist spread his arms. "The difference is irrelevant. I merely need a nice, healthy specimen."

Henry fidgeted. "The fact of the matter is, Mr. Holmquist—"

"Yes?"

"Well, I haven't any frogs. Or toads. They're hard to keep alive in captivity. Won't eat anything but fresh flies or mosquitoes. And I really haven't all day to be catching either for them."

"What kind of a zoo do you keep, Henry?" Holmquist bore down on the cringing man.

"A frogless and toadless one, sir."

Holmquist waved Henry from his presence. "Daltons!"

Fitz and Nelly, following the confrontation with interest, stepped forward. "Yes, sir?"

"I won't need you this morning. Fetch me some frogs. By noon."

The twins shared a glance of disbelief. Fitz spoke first. "Certainly, sir. But frogs usually live around water. Can someone drive us to the closest marsh?"

Holmquist's eyes darted around the set, lighting on the nearest body. "Panther. No, you won't do. I need you for some follow-up shots." He completed the circle. "Schmidt. Your scenes are finished. Do you drive?"

Schmidt gave a sharp nod.

"Good. Take my Packard. Deal with it."

As Fitz and Nelly trailed off the set after Schmidt, Holmquist shouted after them, "And no mud on the leather upholstery, for heaven's sake!"

Fitz and Nelly both filed into the backseat of the automobile and watched Schmidt fuss with the clutch. Nelly prodded her brother and whispered in his ear. "It's still there, you see? Over the right ear. The hair is crimped, as though it'd been burned. The way mine used to look when I was about six and Ma used those wretched curling irons on me. It could be from getting caught near an exploding incendiary bomb. The Jersey City sabotage. Remember?"

"There are problems?" Schmidt asked suspiciously as he conquered the clutch and the engine jerked to life.

"We were just wondering if you'd had an accident, Mr. Schmidt," Nelly answered, all innocence. "Burns to the head can be dangerous. I could borrow some of my mother's special salve for you if you'd like—"

"Is nothing," he growled. "I get too close to the frying sausage, is all."

"Well, then. Do you know of any good marshes?" Fitz smoothly changed the subject as he nudged his sister into silence.

Schmidt grunted. "By Black Tom. Formerly Black Tom. Plenty mosquitoes, plenty frogs. Is good marsh."

Nelly's eyes met her brother's, but neither said a word.

"I think that hair business is a non-clue." Fitz was shoving rushes out of their path. "Too hard to prove, even if he was away from the studio that day. He probably just drank too much beer with Panther's 'aspirin' money and really frizzled himself at the stove, the way he said . . . But Schmidt was certainly right about the mosquitoes." He halted their progress to bat at the steady drone around his ears.

Nelly glanced behind. "Isn't he going to help? He's

still standing on dry ground, twenty yards back . . . Mr. Schmidt?"

Schmidt raised a hand. "I drive, you fetch."

"Well!" Nelly squished past a clump of cattails taller than herself. "Remind me to be stranded on a desert island with that one."

"Not bloody likely." Fitz should have been looking down for leaping amphibians, but instead his attention kept wandering over the desolate landscape before them. "The swamp certainly has taken over what's left of the promontory, hasn't it. Only two years, and all the half-burned sheds have caved in."

Nelly had to stand on tiptoe to follow his eyes over the cattails beginning to close in on them. "There used to be scores of buildings out there. And piers. And Daddy practically in charge of it all—" She tripped and stumbled to a knee in the muck.

"Steady on, Sis. This is probably why Ma never let us come out here. Bad memories."

Nelly rubbed at her eyes with a muddy hand, then slid again. "Ooh. If Cedric Holmquist really knew what he was asking!"

"Yes, well, maybe we'd better find him his stupid frog, then get out of here."

But frogs, even when found, were not that easy to catch. Not for city dwellers. Fitz lunged at several, only to have them slither from his grasp. "Wait, Nell. There's a really tremendous fellow. Hopping that away."

Fitz disappeared through the jungle of reeds and marsh grass in pursuit, leaving Nelly hiking up her skirts to wipe ineffectively at mud-caked stockings. When she heard footsteps slurshing through the muck, it took too long to realize they were coming from the wrong direction.

"Fitz! What are you doing? Fitz . . . !" A strong shove toppled her. A heavy weight ground into her neck.

"Nell! Nell, I got him! Safely wiggling in my pocket. Biggest darn frog you ever saw! Nell?" Fitz stumbled over his sister's body and with horror pulled her lolling head from several inches of ooze. Fingers shaking, he cleared her nose and mouth.

"Nell. Speak to me, Nelly!"

5

A Race for Life

Saved from horrendous subterranean terrors by the timely
arrival of her stouthearted brother, Fitz, Nelly Dalton
escapes with one new piece to the jigsaw of their mystery:
the Kaiser's mastermind of sabotage in America is known
as the *Dark Invader*. Refreshed by smelling salts, Nelly
gamely races with Fitz to catch Lieutenant Lloyd Wright.
Their critical information must be imparted before Wright
ships out to sea.
—"This Week at the Serials," *Moving Picture World*

Dorothy Dalton removed her spectacles to stare somewhat
myopically at her daughter. "I'm not at all certain we
ought to proceed with this serial business . . ."

At the moment, Nelly was far from certain herself.
Muck-covered from head to toe, what she really needed
was the comfort of her mother's arms around her.
Smelling and looking like a wraith from beneath the
swamps, however, she was unsure how to achieve that
desired effect. The less squeamish Fangs whimpered and
began to lick at her closest leg. Meanwhile Fitz, equally
uncomfortable, rocked in his muddy brogans, trying to
explain things.

"It was the frog, Mother. And Holmquist *was* happy

with the specimen I caught. Luckily, he didn't inspect his Packard before we decamped from the studio . . ."

Mrs. Dalton reached for her daughter, mud and all. "You poor dear. Where to begin? A hot tub again, I suppose." She led Nelly down the hall to the tiny bathroom, shutting Fitz outside. "You may explain further through the door, Fitzhugh. Although how you ever allowed your sister to come to this state—"

"It wasn't my fault, Mother! Nelly was shoved. Even stomped on. Hard! Schmidt was the only one around, but he hadn't even a speck of swamp on him when we staggered back to the automobile. Not a speck! I just don't understand—"

Mrs. Dalton raised her voice over the running water. "I've warned you children about the danger of hoboes. Now maybe you'll believe me. Traipsing unattended into the marshes—their very lairs! . . . Clean your shoes in the kitchen, Fitz. And you'd better change your clothes, too. Between this event and all your collars stained with greasepaint, the laundry bill is going to be horrendous this week."

Nelly was back in form by Monday morning, with only a few aching muscles to attest to her real-life adventure. It was fortunate, because she hadn't anticipated Cedric Holmquist's newest trial for her.

"I have to *what?*"

"Learn to drive an automobile, Miss Dalton. It should not be too hard for a young lady of your background."

"What background?"

"The mansion, the pampered upbringing, the steady diet of tutors and such—"

"That's in the *script,* Mr. Holmquist."

"Yes, but a fine actress is expected to rise to the script, Miss Dalton." Holmquist turned to Fitz. "An actor, too, for that matter. However, since your escapade on Friday, it occurred to me that Mr. Schmidt might not be the most felicitous instructor for the purpose. Neither would my Packard be the best vehicle."

He paused to eye the twins. "Have you any idea how long it took to eradicate the marsh from my upholstery? Still, one must pay for Art, I suppose." Holmquist fussed with the collar of his Byronic shirt, then returned to the matter in hand. "Accordingly, Pathmark has made available a Model T and a driver. One Billy Drummond, I believe. You'll find him waiting outside. You may inform Mr. Drummond I expect miracles by 2:00 P.M."

Drummond was napping in the front of a Ford that had seen better days. Fitz tapped him on the shoulder and stood back while the man unfolded himself from the car.

"Well, now. You two would be my new students." He removed a grease-stained cap and smoothed down the few strands of hair arranged strategically across his pate while he considered the twins. "Don't appear too hopeless. Don't even look hysterical like the melodrama star they give me last week. Had vapors just sitting behind the steering wheel, that one did."

"We'll try our best, Mr. Drummond," Fitz finally managed. Truth to tell, he was as unsure as Nelly about their latest assignment. He inspected the vehicle, touching its black paint tentatively. At least it wasn't a horse. Horses tended to stomp and bite.

"Won't get nowhere admiring the finish, son. Come around front here for Lesson Number One."

Fitz followed, Nelly a step behind. Drummond held up an angled piece of iron.

"This here is a crank. Similar to them the cameramen use. To start this buggy, you just insert the crank down here"—he demonstrated—"and add a little muscle power. Give it a try, son, but watch out for the kick."

Some time later, Nelly was sweating profusely inside the cramped cab of the Model T. They hadn't yet moved an inch.

"You got to floor that pedal there, missy, same time you tweak this throttle lever here, right under the steering wheel." Drummond, in the passenger seat, was demonstrating. "It sparks the engine, like I told you before. The automobile don't move lessen you learn to fuss with the throttle easy, whilst you put the engine into proper gear."

"Let me try just once more, Mr. Drummond. I'm sure I'll get the knack this time." She prayed silently, then yelled out, "Give it another crank, Fitz!"

Fitz gave it another crank. Nelly shoved the throttle lever, floored a pedal, and the motor sprang to life.

"Yes! I did it!" In her enthusiasm, Nelly's right foot jammed into the high-speed pedal and the Ford lurched off, narrowly avoiding her startled brother.

"The brake, Missy! Use the brake pedal!"

Nelly was flustered. There were three pedals beneath her foot, after all. She pounded on a random one harder. The Model T continued to jerk forward with enthusiasm. Fitz jumped onto the running board, still flourishing the engine crank. "You nearly mowed me down, Sis!"

Drummond reached frantically for the hand brake and managed to grasp it just before the Model T's front fender broadsided the studio building. The engine sputtered to a halt. Drummond wiped his brow and considered the bare inches between the vehicle and the large PATHMARK STUDIOS sign boldly painted in front of their noses. He finally turned to Nelly.

"While you ain't exactly a hysteric like that melodrama female, I judge it time to turn over the automobile to your brother."

It was decided that Fitz would drive during the racing scene down to the Hudson River. It was actually to be a chase, for, unknown to the hero and heroine, the Dark Invader was pursuing them in *his* automobile, anxious to stop them before they made contact with Lieutenant Wright. Logistically, this meant there was an entire caravan of studio vehicles on the road, the others containing the cameraman, Cedric Holmquist, and assorted crew members.

Midway through the scene, as the automobiles hurled around steep curves of the switchback road working down the side of the Palisades, Holmquist began shouting frantically through his megaphone. No one could hear him over the engine noises, so the chase continued.

Nelly was cringing in the passenger seat next to her

brother, unconvinced by his slapdash driving style that Billy Drummond's lessons had been fully assimilated.

"The brake, Fitz!" she screamed as he headed for another curve. "You do remember where the brake is?"

Fitz grinned. "You're the one who forgot, Nell. Relax. This is fun!"

Nelly clutched the door handle, ready to make an emergency exit. Blaring horns from behind distracted her. She just managed to rip her eyes from the windshield to crane her head backwards. "It's Holmquist. He's banging on the horn, and waving like a madman. I think he wants us to stop."

Fitz did remember where the brake was. He used it. "Too bad," he sighed. "I was just building a little speed."

Nelly chose not to answer. Instead, she gratefully pried open the door and wobbled onto the narrow gravel road. She made it all the way from the sheltering wall of the bluff to the river side, then drew back, aghast.

"It's right down there! The Hudson! And cliffs plunging into it a mere yard from our automobile!"

Holmquist was striding over, oblivious to the dangers at hand. "Dalton! I've just had an inspiration! What we need is a little more excitement in this scene. I'm instructing Schmidt to ram you from behind—that is, to *seem* to ram you, of course. It will look as if your vehicle is making straight for the edge of the Palisades, to be lost forever." The director paused to rub his hands gleefully. "Is that a great new cliff-hanger of an ending, or what?"

Fitz caught Nelly as she began to raise a fist belligerently in Holmquist's direction. "Nix it, Sis," he hissed.

"But he *deserves* to go over the Palisades himself. The man is a menace!"

"He's still our meal ticket."

Luckily for Nelly, the beaming Holmquist returned to his Packard only to discover it had developed a flat tire.

"Zounds!" He kicked at it.

Leaving Nelly still seething well away from the cliff's edge, Fitz walked over to inspect the problem. "Mr. Drummond included tire-changing in his lessons, sir. We should be able to deal with that in no time at all. Where's your spare tube?"

Holmquist kicked again, then hopped impotently on one foot. "At home. It's at home, confound it! I cleaned the entire car after that swamp business and forgot to put it back."

Sam the cameraman stoically began dismantling his equipment. The chase scene was finished for the day.

"Soup *again?*" Fitz replaced the pot's lid, shaking his head.

"But a different kind. Pea soup, dear." Mrs. Dalton was trying to type the last few words of a scene before dinner. Her hands banged over the keys with a final flourish as her head rose. "It's so easy to fix, and so inexpensive. Somehow we don't seem to be saving as much for the winter as I'd hoped."

Fitz glared at the lounging German Shepherd as if to point out the true culprit of the financial situation. "My entire week's salary," he groused. "For the pleasure of 'buying out' this beast's contract!"

Fangs grinned.

"Besides"—Mrs. Dalton hurried to remove the onus from the animal's head—"you know I never really enjoyed laboring over a hot stove, Fitz."

"Poor Ma." Nelly gave her a hug. "We always had Rosie to do the cooking before Dad—"

"I guess I miss Rosie's biscuits the most." Fitz smoothly changed the direction of the conversation. "We've got a recipe for them somewhere, haven't we? Maybe Nell and I could give it a try."

"You'd be willing to *cook,* Fitz?"

"What's so shocking about me cooking, Ma? Some of the world's best chefs are men. Remember the time Dad took us to Delmonico's to celebrate your anniversary? Male cooks. The entire kitchen. Anyhow, you could use a little help, Mother dear."

Dorothy Dalton had just begun to glow with pleasure when Fitz spoiled it all by adding, "I don't think Dad married you for your hidden culinary talents."

"Fitz," Nelly broke in. "Fitz. I think it's time we told Ma about our driving lessons."

"The studio is giving you driving lessons? I thought surely they'd use a stunt artist for those chase scenes I wrote. My, how useful. And how educational!"

Nelly almost added, "And how dangerous," but bit her tongue instead. Best to allow Mother her ivory tower—a nice, safe ivory tower where her scripts couldn't possibly have any connection to reality.

On the morrow, Holmquist decided that Fitz and Nelly would really be shown to better advantage driving an open touring car. That meant the chase scenes had to be retaken, from the top.

"Wow! A six-cylinder Briscoe! With the cyclops-eye headlight!" Fitz circumnavigated the machine half a dozen times before finally letting himself into the driver's side and bouncing on the upholstery. "Sure beats the Model T's springs, too."

Nelly glanced out of the posh vehicle, focusing on more relevant concerns. "By 'from the top,' did Holmquist have to mean the top of the cliffs? Again?"

"Stop complaining, Nelly. I'm trying to figure out the gears. They're more complicated than in that Ford."

"Great. Now you notice. You could've taken it up with Mr. Drummond back at the studio—"

"He was busy with his melodrama star again. And I couldn't mention it to Mr. Holmquist. *He* was busy trying to deal with Henry's convulsions over those giant cockroaches."

Nelly shuddered in remembrance. "It was more than disgusting. Peeking into their little cage and finding only empty carapaces . . ."

"Not all empty. The survivor was fat and happy enough."

"Yuck. One blissful, bloated giant cockroach. And Henry ripping out his hair by the fistfuls . . ."

"Are we ready, Daltons?" Cedric Holmquist's voice wafted forward from his megaphone. "Start your engine!"

Three harrowing days later, Nelly and Fitz finally made it down to the Hudson River in their touring car. Lloyd Wright was patiently waiting in his spotless, crisply creased uniform, as though he and the entire U.S. Navy had nothing better to do with themselves than attend to the Daltons' latest clues. Although the actual arrival at water's edge was no longer in the current episode, the director had decided to shoot it anyway, as the beginning of the next.

Somewhere along the way, Nelly decided that God must surely have a special place in His heart for serial stars. Having accepted that benign protection as a given, she relaxed and watched Schmidt try to kill her brother and herself.

And Schmidt did try. He drove like one either drunk or insane. Possibly both. The rear of the Briscoe was much the worse for its collisions with Schmidt's devil car, but strangely enough, each bump and scrape seemed to move Holmquist to new heights of praise for the German.

"Did you ever see such driving?" he gushed over and over. "Such precision. Such sheer, malicious artistry!" And finally, safely on the banks of the Hudson River, "You've earned yourself a bonus, Schmidt!"

As usual, Schmidt was unmoved by the praise. Since the frog incident—there really hadn't been a hobo camp in sight—Nelly had been rapidly reassessing her opinion of the man. Her current impressions were nowhere near as broad-minded as her earlier ones. She was now fairly certain Schmidt would have truly preferred the touring car—and its occupants—several leagues beneath the waters of the mighty river. The question in her mind was *why?*

6

The Aerial Peril

A single tire caught upon a gnarled tree saves Fitzhugh and
Nelly Dalton from crashing to oblivion over the Palisades.
In the nick of time they reach Lieutenant Wright, who
arranges to have his orders changed. He will personally fly
the accumulated information to Washington, D.C., taking
the intrepid twins—with their guardian's consent—as ver-
ification before the Secret Service.
    —"This Week at the Serials," *Moving Picture World*

"No. Absolutely not!"

"What are you nattering on about, Nell?"

Another rainy Sunday afternoon had the Dalton family imprisoned in their kitchen. It was even getting to
Fangs. Now it was the dog who leaned paws upon the
windowsill, staring into the rain rustling through the
apple tree.

"I'm not nattering, Fitz. I'm adamant. I will *not* take
flying lessons. I won't even get into—"

"I do believe I directed in the script that Lieutenant
Wright should appear to do whatever aeroplane flying is
necessary, dear."

"Ma's right. And Lloyd's even been taking proper

lessons." Fitz's envy was apparent. "When he passes and finishes our serial, he intends to join up with the American Expeditionary Forces overseas. He's got his sights set on the Lafayette Escadrille, lucky dog."

Nelly paced around the kitchen table. "I don't care what you say, or what Mother says. By this time I think I know Cedric Holmquist. *He'll* find a way to get me into that aeroplane, all right. And then he'll make it *crash*!"

"Where's your artistic spirit, Sis? A true actress takes anything in stride, overcomes all plot complications for the good of the piece."

Nelly turned on her brother. "I'm becoming quite a good actress, thank you, but I fail to see how much emoting I can do in an aeroplane several thousand feet up in the sky!"

"Now, Nelly dear, you know a real aeroplane isn't truly called for. A mock-up will do just fine for the scenes I've written. Then Mr. Holmquist can use some old newsreel footage for the actual scenes in the air—"

"It won't work out like that, Mother." Nelly flounced into a chair. "Dear Cedric will find something unartistic about using someone else's shots and—"

"Do settle down, Nelly." Mrs. Dalton was beginning to lose her patience. "Fitz, find the deck of cards. You could play a few hands of rummy."

Fitz didn't move.

"Then again, you could both read a book. That would be even more peaceful."

Dorothy Dalton sighed at the total lack of enthusiasm her suggestions inspired. Very carefully she wiped her lenses with her shirtwaist blouse. "All right. Why don't you make those biscuits you've been threatening. At least we could eat them."

Fangs became the recipient of most of the biscuits. They'd been left in the oven a trifle overlong. The dog, however, consumed them with evident relish. Full at last, he fetched his leash from the doorknob and nudged Nelly with it.

"It's still raining, Fangs." Nelly stopped rubbing silver polish from the carefully embossed BLACK TOM SECURITY of her father's badge long enough to glance out the window. "In point of fact, it's pouring."

"Fangs does need his constitutional before bedtime. You've polished at that badge enough. Why you insist on wearing it nearly every day evades me."

"It makes me feel good, Ma. Besides, I don't have any other jewelry."

Fitz inspected the sink filled with mixing bowls and utensils and groaned. "After his walk, I won't have the energy to wash up."

"Then you may stay and wash up, Fitz. I'll walk Fangs."

"Hey! I'm not sure that's a fair trade—"

But Nelly was already at the door and grabbing for the umbrella. "Ta!"

Outside, Fangs pursued his usual course down the street past the two- and three-story frame houses with their tidy, grassy yards to the more open park at the end of the block. There Nelly unclasped his leash and let him roam through the wet darkness at his leisure. She waited for the dog to return until stealthy footsteps from out of nowhere made her twist around beneath her umbrella.

"Never creep up on me like that, Fitz. It's scary . . ." She squinted through the blackness. The hulking, raincoat-shrouded figure closing in on her certainly wasn't Fitz. "Fangs!" she screamed out as a gloved hand reached for her.

Almost instantly the animal appeared, and with a leap of massive proportions he sprang at Nelly's masked attacker. The fierce growl emanating from Fangs's throat was echoed by a hoarse shriek as teeth met body. Nelly gasped, frozen, and stood watching with fascination as her protector wrestled with the assailant. It was an uneven battle, and finally it was enough, even for her.

"Fangs! Heel!"

Snapping his powerful jaws a final time, Fangs backed off, bristles raised along his spine. The masked man crawled a few feet before laboriously righting himself. Limping, raincoat in shreds, he fled silently into the trees.

Nelly shook with a sudden palsy until Fangs gave a questioning yip. She bent to embrace her dog. "Good boy!" Nelly removed a scrap of torn cloth from his mouth and shoved it absentmindedly into a pocket. "*Wonderful* boy! But I think it's time to go home."

Nelly stood to peer around the deserted park. She folded her arms against her body, trying to stop the shivers. The dark blob of trees she would have to pass loomed large and forbidding, an obstacle suddenly become more threatening than the sheer cliffs of the Palisades. She took several deep breaths until she finally felt capable of moving. "We'll bring Fitz along next time, Fangs."

"You really ought to have told Ma, Nelly."

The twins were walking to the studio the next morning.

"I mean, she ought to be forewarned. In case she goes out by herself—"

It was a warm morning, but Nelly felt cold as they walked past the trees of the little park. "Mother only goes out during the day for marketing, Fitz. And she always takes Fangs along. First there was that 'hobo' business at Black Tom. There was no way we could hide that from her . . . Now this. If she knew about last night, she'd be moving us again, and not just to Mrs. Bernini's third floor. I don't have the energy to keep moving all the time, Fitz. We need to take a stand somewhere . . . Besides, I have a feeling it's you and me this, this *villain* is after. Specifically."

Fitz ran fingers through his thick blond hair distractedly. "But why, Nell? Why? We're just fifteen. What do we have that this lowlife could want?"

"We haven't anything, really. We both realize that. Maybe the question should be, what do we *know?*"

Fitz jammed his hands into his pockets. "Whatever it is, I'd certainly like the answer to that one myself . . . What could we know that's worth resorting to violence to learn? The current violence in the world is three thousand miles away in Europe. Except for occasional sabotage right here in Jersey. And all we really know about that is Dad's shopping list, and maybe other notes hidden somewhere."

"Fat lot of good any of that has done us."

Fitz pulled out a hand, still balled up, and shook it.

"We also have an unknown snooper and maybe even a newspaper reporter trying to track us. Then there's Schmidt attacking that beautiful automobile—"

"With us in it," Nelly clarified.

"With us in it. As if he really wanted it over the cliffs. Even if it was on Holmquist's orders—" Fitz spread his fingers as if grasping for a truth, even a small one. Not having one at hand, he settled for a decision. "We're going to have to go on alert, Nell. We may be at war ourselves. And for a starter we should see if our Mr. Schmidt shows any signs of recently having escaped from the clutches of an outraged dog."

"Like a sudden limp?"

"Precisely," he agreed.

At the studio the two split to search for Schmidt. Fitz gave up first. "I don't think he was scheduled to shoot today, Nell."

"Just our luck. When we finally had a really good clue, too."

Fitz shrugged. "Looks like Holmquist has another excursion organized, anyway."

Nelly immediately forgot Schmidt as she took in the director's aviator outfit. It was going to happen, just as she'd suspected all along.

"Into the automobiles, my chickadees. We're off to the aerodrome. The skies are clear and it's a lovely day for flying!"

Happily, the day was far less strenuous than Nelly had feared. There were a number of background shots to be photographed: the small field itself, really not much more than an open meadow muddy from the rains of the previous day; the wooden shack with its observation tower jutting twenty feet above it; the bright colors of a wind sleeve billowing in the breeze; the handful of cheerfully painted single-engine aeroplanes scattered across the field. Worry as she might, none of this made Nelly feel threatened. Slowly the anxieties of the previous night began to ease away. The bright planes were like fairy-tale characters optimistically promising a happy ending. The world of movie make-believe could become addictive.

Long and medium shots were set up around a single-engine biplane. Lloyd Wright twirled the wooden propeller of the "Jenny" training plane dashingly. Fitz and Nelly admired Lloyd grinning without a care in the front cockpit, the young aviator off to conquer the sky. They were all storybook characters, all larger than life.

When Holmquist finally ordered it, Nelly actually enjoyed squeezing into the rear cockpit with her brother to blow exuberant farewell kisses at Paul Panther. The engine was blessedly silent, after all. And the soft leather helmet she was given to wear made her feel like a true aviatrix. She could even harbor illusions about actually taking the throttle in hand and lifting the pretty bird into the blue heavens herself.

Later, after Holmquist was satisfied with his setup shots, there were fun and games, picnicking on blankets near the sheltering wings of the Jenny. Paul Panther, his usual trim suit jacket and vest discarded, snaffled three apples and began to juggle them dexterously. He noticed

Nelly's open-mouthed wonder. "Just something I picked up doing a circus serial with Eddie Polo."

"Stop showing off, Paul!" Lloyd mischievously grabbed one of the apples in mid-flight. "Catch, Nell!"

Nelly managed not to fumble it, then tossed it toward Fitz. In a moment, Sam and even Holmquist were drawn into the game. It spread over the field until one by one they flopped back onto the blankets laughing.

The entire crew motored back to the studio that afternoon bellowing "It's a Long, Long Way to Tipperary." A rare sense of camaraderie had been achieved. But then, Schmidt had been notably absent from the entire affair.

Nelly did get her plane crash on Friday, but it was hardly the event she'd been dreading. She had Pathmark Studios to thank for that.

Holmquist was in a dither when Nelly and Fitz arrived in the morning. He was shaking a directive from the office tower.

"What do they mean, I'm over budget? What do they mean, they aren't approving funds to rent that biplane for actual flight? How do they expect me to make the most exciting serial in motion picture history if they keep plucking my feathers?" He waved the message dramatically at the staring twins. "What, I ask you, *what* does the studio office know about *Art*?"

Fortunately, it was a rhetorical question, because neither Fitz nor Nelly had the answer. Fitz shuffled uncomfortably before finally asking, "How will we do the scene with Nelly hanging from the wings? And me plucking her from oblivion while Lloyd's busy trying to snuff out the engine fire in mid-flight?" He steadied on his feet to continue. "If we can't have an engine fire, what happens to that great piece with the Dark Invader pursuing us like the Red Baron, shooting both his guns? I sort of liked that part."

"*You* sort of liked that part!" Cedric Holmquist was practically raving. "It was brilliant. Overpoweringly brilliant!"

The lowly assistant Ernest edged up to the director, very tentatively. "Mr. Holmquist, sir?"

Holmquist practically shoved his Adam's apple down the young man's throat. Ernest's bow tie trembled. "What is it? Can't you see I'm busy seething at life's injustices?"

"Yes, sir, but, well . . . there might be a solution."

Holmquist backed off an inch. "A solution? Speak!"

Fitz was seated in the rear cockpit of the solution, an aeroplane mock-up Ernest had borrowed from a feature-length war drama currently shooting at the far end of the studio. Nelly was draped artfully over a wing, clutching at struts with both fists, feet kicking helplessly, her skirts billowing in the ferocious air currents being produced by a giant fan just off set.

"Glance down!" Holmquist bellowed through his megaphone over the drone of the fan. "Glance down ever so briefly, Miss Dalton. Register the full thousand feet between your dangling legs and the earth below!"

A technician to Nelly's left levered the fake plane body into a dramatic, plunging position, while another frantically cranked a moving backdrop of sky, clouds, and birds behind her. Nelly glanced down and gasped. Should she relinquish her hold on the struts she would fall to certain death—all four feet to the studio floor. Not momentous perhaps, but the solid concrete might smart a little . . . Then again, maybe it was time to utilize her blossoming acting skills.

"Fitz!" she pleaded. "Fitz, save me!"

Fitz was struggling from the cockpit, one hand stretching to grasp for hers. "Let go of the strut, Nelly! I'll save you! . . . No! No! Not both hands at once!"

Nelly fell with a thud and Holmquist screeched "Cut!" and stormed over.

"That was the silliest thing I ever saw. What kind of heroine would let go with *both* hands in midair while trying to hang on to a plummeting aircraft?"

"A *dumb* heroine, Mr. Holmquist." Nelly was angrily rearranging her skirt over a bruised knee. That concrete was even harder than she'd estimated. Some of Holmquist's stupidity must be rubbing off onto her. "Only a half-wit would keep running off to certain death, week after week. That's what you've got, isn't it? And that's what your audience expects. I was merely trying to keep in character."

"Break!" yelled the director, eyeball to eyeball with Nelly. "Our heroine needs a short rest to rethink her priorities. Lloyd! You may stop hovering around Miss Dalton so solicitously. Any damage she's incurred is deserved. We'll move on to the next set and do you thrashing with the fire. Schmidt! Good to have you back again. Stick around. We still need those close-ups of you bearing down to destroy the good guys with your guns."

By late afternoon it was Holmquist who had done most of the rethinking regarding Nelly's outburst.

"In retrospect, Miss Dalton . . . in retrospect, perhaps you made a useful point. The falling scene as currently shot would make an excellent conclusion to Episode Six. We needn't actually show the aircraft itself crashing— thereby saving the cost of rebuilding the contraption. Mr. Morris should be pleased by that little economy."

The director smirked at his cleverness. "Then we can just open Episode Seven with your brother's arm shooting out and plucking you from thin air. Yes, I do like that." Holmquist turned from Nelly with a wave of his arm. "You are dismissed, Miss Dalton. Not a bad week's work."

7

Terror Train

Nelly is grasped from a plunging death by her quick-witted brother, Fitzhugh. Alas, thanks to the Dark Invader, Lieutenant Wright's plane is permanently disabled. The threesome return to the Dalton mansion to lick their wounds and consult with the twins' guardian. Panther emphasizes the need for a speedy trip to Washington and recommends the evening train.
— "This Week at the Serials," *Moving Picture World*

"Your plot needs justification, Ma. Why are we so anxious to get to Washington with so little real evidence?"

The Daltons were out for a Saturday evening stroll with Fangs. The summer heat had become oppressive, and their apartment was a hot box. Now they were extending the walk as long as possible, none of them anxious to return.

"It's a device known as a *red herring,* Fitz. Writers have been using it for some time." Mrs. Dalton stopped to untangle the dog's leash from her legs. "I believe it actually derives from the old English practice of dragging a herring across a trail to confuse hunting hounds."

"A sort of false clue, Ma?" Fitz pressed.

"Well, that's one interpretation. I've chosen to use it in its broader sense."

"So it's really to distract attention from the true issue, then?" Nelly bent down to unclasp Fangs's leash. "You'd never let a smelly old dead fish confuse you, would you, boy?"

Fangs wriggled in her embrace and barked a quick no.

"He's tired of being led. Have you got that tennis ball, Fitz? Let's teach him how to fetch."

"Around the corner at the park, Nell." He hesitated in swift remembrance of his sister's recent experience there. "Unless you think it might be getting too dark. Or the ball might get lost in the trees . . ."

Dorothy Dalton, unburdened by her children's knowledge, removed her straw hat and used its brim to fan herself. "Nonsense. The park sounds lovely. I'll just sit under one of those huge trees and watch."

Nelly rubbed sudden perspiration from both temples as she met her brother's eyes. "I guess it's the park, then."

The heat broke in a series of daylong thundershowers on Monday. Holmquist kept staring at the rain pummeling the studio skylights and muttering, "It *never* rains in California!" In between complaints, he oversaw the special-effects staff as they conjured up a train wreck for Episode Seven of *In the Kaiser's Clutch*.

Fitz was fascinated by the miniature railroad. He hung over the broad table on which it was set, hounding the "engineers" with questions.

"Has it got a real little engine inside? . . . You aren't truly going to destroy it, are you? . . . If you do, will it be over that trestle bridge, into the river below? . . . Or will it be a head-on collision?"

The technician in charge finally dragged his attention from the models. "If I'm going for a special effect, pal, I want to make it as special as possible. When this baby goes up in smoke, it'll be from a massive, head-on collision, in the direct *center* of the trestle bridge. Boom. Down will come baby, cradle, and all."

"Wow."

Nelly nudged her brother. "Come on, Fitz, they're ready to shoot, and you're in Sam's way." But even Nelly couldn't resist pausing for another look at the scenic vistas set around the tiny train tracks. "Mr. Holmquist?"

"What is it, Miss Dalton?"

"It's a lovely set, but isn't the land mostly flat between New York and Washington? This looks like pictures I've seen of the Rocky Mountains. And the scale . . . surely there isn't a railroad bridge with a five-hundred-foot drop anywhere nearby on the East Coast. There wasn't the time our father took us to Washington to see the Capitol and the White House. Remember, Fitz?"

Holmquist frowned for only a brief moment. "A mere bagatelle, Miss Dalton. If there isn't, there *ought* to be, at least in our serial." He turned to the cameraman. "Are we ready, Sam? Do try to get it in one take. Special effects are so expensive these days."

After shooting farewell scenes at the local railway station for most of Tuesday, Fitz and Nelly were eager to head home, when they overheard Holmquist proffer an unexpected invitation to their "guardian."

"The first two episodes have been edited and titled, Panther. Care to screen them with me tonight?"

Panther was nodding an acceptance when he noticed the twins. "How about including the kids, Cedric? They'd enjoy it."

Holmquist had the grace to look only slightly put out. "Of course, Daltons . . . Your lovely mother, too. She *was* responsible for the screenplays."

"Golly! Do you mean it, Mr. Holmquist? I thought we'd have to wait till *Clutch* played at the local Bijou!"

Nelly was excited, too, but she felt her brother's display was a little excessive. "We'd be happy to come, Mr. Holmquist. What time?"

"Shall we say eight? In the studio screening room?"

Of necessity, Fangs was left home after a light supper was consumed. The dog had never before been abandoned, and was not pleased when he caught on. Nelly had to restrain him at the apartment door.

"Stay, Fangs. Be good. You're our guard dog, after all, and it's your job to protect the home fires in our absence."

Fangs wuffled pathetically, but obeyed. His mournful howl floated from the open kitchen window to follow them all the way down the street.

Mrs. Dalton patted one of the cabbage-sized roses on her huge hat. "Gracious. I do hope Mrs. Bernini won't be upset by that concert. She has been tremendously understanding about the dog. Maybe I should go back—"

"Nonsense." Fitz took his mother's arm. "He'll stop in a few minutes, and you wouldn't want to miss our premiere!"

Pathmark Studios' product may have been cheap, but its screening room had luxuriously appointed seats and a lush carpet. It even had a curtained screen, just as in one of the better movie houses. It also was filled with smoke from the cigars of Paul Panther and an assortment of studio personnel. Cedric Holmquist, however, was puffing on a very British-looking pipe, the obvious accessory to his velvet smoking jacket.

Mrs. Dalton accepted a nod from Holmquist and a courtly bow from Panther and proceeded to wave a path through the reeking fumes with her handkerchief. "Where shall we sit, Fitz? In the front row by the piano? Do you suppose there will actually be an accompanist?"

"I think not at this stage, Mother. It's not as if our picture were a feature."

"Well, then"—she settled into a seat, carefully shoving a nearby ashtray aside—"we'll just have to imagine our own music until we can hear it in a real theater." She pulled out a long hatpin and removed her flowered extravaganza, placing it in her lap. "Come sit by my side, Nelly."

Holmquist turned to the glassed-in projection booth near the rear ceiling of the small room. "Ready when you are, up there!"

Lights dimmed and the first title reached the screen. It was a lurid caricature of Kaiser Wilhelm—spiked helmet and all—gripping a map of America in his hands. Super-imposed over this was the credit information:

IN THE KAISER'S CLUTCH
A Serial in Fifteen Episodes
Episode One:
Caught in the Web

The words scrolled up the screen to be replaced with:

Directed by Cedric Holmquist
Starring Paul Panther and Lloyd Wright
Introducing the Dalton Twins

"We ought to get better billing than that," Fitz muttered under his breath. "At least first names! We are doing most of the work—"

"Ssh!" Nelly hissed. "Lloyd Wright and Panther have been in serials forever." She settled back to watch a tennis match fill the screen.

Forty minutes and the first two completed episodes later the lights came up again. Nelly was in shock. "Did you see me all covered with cobwebs? And practically drowning in that fake submarine!"

"How about that fistfight with Schmidt," Fitz was enthusing. "Did I look professional, or what? I think I'll go out for the boxing team at school this winter."

Mrs. Dalton still had her hands primly folded over her massive hat. "Well. You certainly both appeared considerably older than fifteen."

"Is that all you've got to say, Mother?"

It was all she had a chance to say. Holmquist was bustling over. "What do you think of your new stars, Mrs. Dalton? Were they not most effectively directed? And more photogenic than one could have hoped. Yes"— he poked happily at the bowl of his pipe—"I can foresee the studio renewing their contracts in the fall."

Dorothy Dalton rose from her seat with dignity. "That remains to be seen. Thank you for a most instructive evening, Mr. Holmquist . . . Come along, children, you've work in the morning."

Fitz was in a combative mood all the way home. "How could you call us *children* right in front of our director, Mother?"

"Because that's what you still are, no matter what tricks Mr. Holmquist chooses to play with my script." She shoved her lethal hatpin decisively through a pink rose. If it had been Holmquist, he would have been skewered. "I don't care to see you used. Nelly looking ten years older with all that makeup, and practically bare in that tub of water—"

"I did have on a bathing costume underneath, Mother."

"But entirely too much was left to the imagination . . . And all of it shot fully within the sight of that nice young man Lloyd Wright, not to mention Paul Panther. What could they be thinking of you!" She picked up her stride, and Nelly and Fitz had to trot to catch up with her.

"You *wrote* me into that water, Ma!"

Mrs. Dalton slowed down. "I'm fully aware of that. Oh,

dear, I never thought I'd be selling my own children to survive. If your poor father were only alive—"

"He'd be walking along with us, Ma, chuckling," Fitz broke in. "He had a pretty good sense of humor. And he always treated us as if we were already fully grown."

Dorothy Dalton raised her head to inspect the son towering over her. "You are growing, Fitz. I won't dispute that, and I am trying to deal with it. I just wish you weren't being rushed to complete maturity by this moving picture business. Innocence is such a precious commodity . . . and so short-lived."

They reached their house and climbed to the second floor in silence. Mrs. Dalton, still upset, shoved the key in the lock and pushed the door open. Then she screamed.

"I can't believe it!" Nelly was comforting a bristling Fangs amid the wreckage of their kitchen-sitting room. Chairs and books were strewn everywhere, their father's violin case rakishly balanced on edge atop them. Even the kitchen table had been overturned to lie on its side among broken shards of supper dishes.

Dorothy Dalton was leaning against the closest wall. "Could Fangs have done all this in an hour and a half?"

"Fangs wasn't responsible for this, Mother." Fitz was holding up a scrap of bloodied cloth. He walked slowly with it in hand to the still-open kitchen window, where he thoughtfully gazed out past the few red drops speckled on the sill. "The apple tree's been messed with, too. The closest branch has been snapped off. And I can bet there'll be a lot of green apples on the ground in the morning."

Nelly let go of the heaving dog. "Let me see that cloth, Fitz." She inspected it by the light of the ceiling lamp. "It looks a lot like that other scrap from last week."

Mrs. Dalton took a deep breath and pushed herself away from the wall. "*What* other scrap? What happened last week?"

Fitz glanced at his sister. "Ma's right, Nell. Innocence is short-lived. Maybe in return for asking her to treat us as adults we should treat our mother the same way."

Fitz and Nelly sleepily picked their way through leftover detritus to the kitchen table the next morning. In a loose chenille robe, unbound hair flowing richly down her back, Dorothy Dalton was scrambling eggs at the stove. "At least our intruder was kind enough to keep out of the icebox."

Fitz pulled broad red suspenders over his shoulders, poured a glass of milk from the pitcher, and began lavishly buttering a piece of toast. "He never made it out of this room, Ma. Fangs saw to that. It must've been one heck of a fight to get everything knocked over like it was." Fitz bent to shove the toast under the table. "Good Fangs. You just paid back your contract price, in spades." Fangs swallowed the offering and licked Fitz's hand.

Mrs. Dalton brought the frying pan to the table, then stood there, staring at the eggs. "I really didn't want to move again. Not until we were ready to go back to New York in September."

Nelly reached for the pan. "Sit down, Ma. I'll pass out the eggs. And I vote that we stay, Dark Invader and all. But we'll have to figure out what's going on."

Dorothy Dalton sat, her elbows on the table, head in her hands. She slowly looked up. "What to do? Can we keep running forever?"

"No!" Fitz swallowed a mouthful of breakfast. "We can't. And I don't think Dad would have wanted us to, either. I vote with Sis."

"Are we operating a family democracy now?"

"Why not, Ma?" Fitz grinned. "It's a free country, and you two women wanted the vote!"

"Perhaps we *should* have called in the police last night," their mother tried. "In spite of everything." Her eyes scanned the disaster area yet again. "It's still not too late. Maybe the Fort Lee police will be more comforting than their New York counterparts. More efficient . . ."

"Less officious?" Nelly offered.

Fitz reached for more toast. "I can bet you even the Fort Lee police would be trailed by a bored reporter or two looking for copy. After that Jersey City explosion, one smart, bored reporter might remember our name and connect us back to Black Tom—"

"And the badgering would start all over again," breathed Mrs. Dalton.

"Right. I really don't see what good it would do, Ma. The only clues our visitor left behind were a few drops of blood and that scrap of cloth, which just happens to be a fair match with Nelly's scrap . . . Whoever was here last night was searching for something—or trying to. *We* don't even know what. Yet somehow I'm beginning to believe this is all tied in with Dad and Black Tom and sabotage."

"Why, Fitz?" his mother asked. "How could it possibly be connected to Black Tom?"

"I can't be sure, Ma, but think back to the first incident."

"The eavesdropper outside the window?" Nelly asked.

"Exactly. We never might have known he was there except that he got excited and bumped his head—"

"—and he bumped his head when we were talking about Dad and his shopping list," Nelly finished.

Mrs. Dalton rubbed her own head distractedly. Nelly sprang from her unfinished eggs to massage her mother's neck. "You're not getting one of your headaches, are you, Ma? In the middle of all this mess?"

"It is a mess, and not just the upturned furniture. I can't help but wish there were someone we could rely on, another adult I could confide in. This whole business shouldn't have to rest solely on my shoulders and those of my two dearest offspring." She straightened those shoulders valiantly. "Off to the studio, both of you. Deal with your movie disasters, and I'll deal with this one."

8
Cave of Despair

The Dalton twins and Lieutenant Wright miraculously survive the disastrous train wreck, but find themselves at the bottom of a ravine, being pursued by their furious, foiled nemesis. Seeking shelter desperately, they scramble up the mountainside to find a hidden cave. Safely inside, they hope to take stock and make plans.
—"This Week at the Serials," *Moving Picture World*

"It's back to the Palisades today, troops." Holmquist searched the faces before him. "Where is that Schmidt? Gone again? I could substitute for him, but his build is so perfect for the Dark Invader—"

"You could ask Mr. Panther, sir. He usually knows." It was the beginning of a fresh week, and Fitz was trying to be helpful.

"Panther's written out of this week's episode. He asked specifically for a break. Some family business." Holmquist shrugged. "I suppose we could get by another day without Schmidt. We'll shoot the climbing and cave interiors. But if he thinks he's getting paid . . ."

Holmquist was distracted by Henry the animal keeper.

"Ah, there you are, Henry. Have you brought our furry friend?"

"Waiting in the truck, Mr. Holmquist, sir. I thought it best not to get him too excited before his actual shots."

"Quite prudent. Come along to manage him, then."

"Manage whom?" That old feeling of foreboding was creeping over Nelly again. "Mother didn't write any creatures into the cave scene—"

"She should have, Miss Dalton. She should have. Interior as well as exterior traumas do tend to build up suspense to a much more believable level." Holmquist patted Nelly lightly on the shoulder. "Not to upset your pretty head. Theodore is a real little teddy bear."

Theodore may have been cuddly, but he was not little. At the base of the Palisades, Nelly watched him being unloaded from his cage. Henry led him down the ramp from the truck, not missing Nelly's guarded interest.

"A genuine American black bear, he is. Caught him in the Adirondacks myself last fall when he wasn't no more than a cub. Not too many of Theodore's kind left." Henry patted the bear's rump fondly. As if on cue, Theodore hoisted himself onto his rear legs and did a clumsy, two-footed dance, grinning all the while.

Nelly was not fooled by the trick. Upright, the monster seemed to tower several feet over her slender frame. She felt quickly in her pocket for a reddening apple she'd picked from their tree that morning. "Good Theodore. Down, boy. Here."

Theodore snatched at the offering with alarmingly

sharp claws, thumped to all fours, and crunched into it, slathering.

Nelly backed away another yard. "How are you going to get him into the cave, Henry?"

"Theodore loves mountains." Henry smiled. "This will be a real treat for him. We'll just amble up ahead of you."

It was not a large cave, but large enough for Holmquist's purposes. Theodore was already tucked into a rear niche, sharing a nap with Henry, when the twins and crew straggled into it, puffing.

Fitz wiped his brow and watched the technicians scowl at the difficulties facing them. "I don't understand, Mr. Holmquist. Couldn't this cave have been made in the studio much more easily? There's no electricity up here for lights, and—"

"That is the problem of the lighting people, Mr. Dalton. They can set off a few charges or something. As for myself, I've always found caves to be much more mysterious and evocative in their native habitat."

Fitz inspected the rough ceiling of rock just barely clearing his head. This time he suppressed a shudder. An avalanche had been scheduled in the script to close off the outside of the cave, imprisoning Nelly and Lloyd Wright and himself within, but *charges* sounded like dynamite. And a little TNT would make mincemeat of this place. The rugged, irregular walls unaccountably began to close in on him.

"Fitz. Fitz, are you all right?" Nelly was at his side.

"It's nothing, Sis . . . But I never thought I'd be claustrophobic."

She grabbed his arm and pulled him out the opening. "I know how you feel. Even snoring, that bear eats up all the space."

They tentatively settled on the rim of the trail just under an overhang a short distance from the mouth of the cave and swung their legs over the precipice. The Hudson River wasn't nearly as far down as it had been from the road during their racing episode, but it was far enough. Nelly briefly peered beyond the edge, then jerked her head quickly back. In an attempt at nonchalance—and to cover the furious pounding of her heart before her brother heard it—she rolled up the embroidered cuffs of her muslin blouse and pulled the sailor collar away from her damp neck.

"Phew. Who'd think it would be so hot halfway down the side of a cliff?" A glance at Fitz told her that neither her nonchalance nor her conversation had been noted. He really had been frightened, probably more by his reaction to the cave than by the cave itself.

Funny things, caves and cliffs. Nothing in their lives up to this point had prepared them for either. There ought to be a class at school for that sort of thing. Also for burglaries and unexpected night assaults. It could be called "A Youth's Companion to the Traumas of Life." It would be infinitely more useful than algebra. Nelly craned her neck around the sheltering ledge to scan the comforting solidity of the Palisades reaching above them. Curiouser and curiouser. A cliff wasn't in the least intimidating from this viewpoint, looking *up*. Her neck inched farther.

"Strange."

Fitz was still busy catching his breath, but he finally registered Nelly's voice. "What's strange?"

"It seems we've got some spectators up there. Way at the top. Several heads keep popping over the edge—"

Fitz didn't even bother looking. "Just kids out of school, wondering what the crazy movie people are doing halfway up the Palisades."

Nelly squinted through the noon haze. "It doesn't look like children. They seem to be yelling at each other, and wrestling over something."

Fitz finally turned and stretched past Nelly to scrutinize the situation for himself. He studied the scene silently from under the tiny ledge protecting them from sight for several long moments, then jerked back, pulling Nelly with him. "Whoever it is, they just shoved a boulder over the side! Right at us!"

It was nearly sunset by the time the studio rescue team, fetched by Fitz and Nelly, broke through the rockslide into the cave.

Holmquist inched out first, stood to brush himself off, then stepped back to inspect the scene through the lens around his neck.

"A pity the light is going. I couldn't have planned a better avalanche myself." He turned with annoyance on the twins. "I suppose we'll have to construct that cave in the studio after all. My cowardly crew swore if they got out alive they'd never set foot near the Palisades again."

"A *what* happened today?" Dorothy Dalton placed a sadly desiccated roast chicken before her children. "And don't you dare say a word about my cooking, Fitzhugh. It was meant to be a special treat. And it would have been, too, if you weren't three hours late to dinner."

Nelly stared at the bird, then at her mother. "Oh, no. It's your birthday!"

Fitz started guiltily. "We really had planned a present, Ma. We nearly had enough saved from our allowances for your ruby earrings."

Mrs. Dalton shrugged and sawed at a chicken leg. The knife finally broke through and she delicately passed the appendage to her son. "Your favorite, Fitz. And the thigh for Nelly . . . At my age, after all, a birthday is only something to survive. Do try not to break any teeth."

In retrospect, the birthday dinner was harder to endure than the twins' adventures that day. Fitz surreptitiously slid his second drumstick under the table. Fangs just as discreetly accepted and devoured it. The dog was developing more useful qualities each day. Fitz drained his glass of milk and cleared his throat. "We got to drive again this afternoon, Ma."

She looked up from her untouched plate. "Yes?"

"Your avalanche scene was more effective than anticipated. Unfortunately, it wasn't scheduled to be shot until Thursday."

Mrs. Dalton stopped toying with her fork. "Perhaps you'd care to explain?"

"Everyone was caught inside the cave, Mother," Nelly began. "Everyone except Fitz and me. We had to scramble down the cliff, start the nearest automobile—"

"It was Holmquist's Packard." Fitz grinned with pleasure. "What a sweet machine!"

"Not after you practically stripped its gears, Fitz."

"Please, children. Could we get to the point?"

"The point was *sabotage.*" Fitz's grin had disappeared. "Nelly and I saw some characters loosen the boulder with our own eyes. And on the way back from reporting the accident to the studio we stopped on top of the cliff, just to be certain it wasn't our imaginations—"

"The serial does get to one that way sometimes, Mother, between your incredible plots and Holmquist's additions—"

"But we were right, Ma," Fitz continued. "We found the exact spot. The ground was different, as if it had been sitting under a huge rock for ages, and only now saw the light of day. Not to mention the trail carved by that boulder bowling down the side of the cliff—"

"—and there were other marks," Nelly finished triumphantly. "The kind of marks a tool like a crowbar would make."

"Well, some of them had been scuffed over, Sis, probably on purpose." Fitz's enthusiasm died. "But not a single piece of evidence we could carry away . . . If we'd only had a camera with us."

Their mother listened to the complete story, her eyes growing larger behind their spectacles. She finally removed the glasses and carefully rubbed the bridge of her nose. "Whom else have you told about this?"

Nelly shrugged. "We started with Enoch Morris, the studio manager. We had to go all the way to him because nobody else would believe us about the avalanche. And even he didn't want the details. He just got all red and chomped his cigar in two and yelled about cursed Huns trying to put him out of business—as if he'd been expecting something like this to happen. We tried with Holmquist, too, after the rescue, but he was in a dither over missing that avalanche shot. Then we tried Sam—"

"—but Sam," Fitz explained, "was practically paralyzed with fright from spending eight hours with Theodore—"

"And who is *Theodore?*"

"An American black bear, Mother. His food was left in the truck at the bottom of the cliff, and after his nap he became a little testy inside the closed cave—"

"Nelly and Fitz." Mrs. Dalton dropped her glasses and reached a hand out to each of them. "There've been too many mysterious incidents in your presence. Swear to me that you won't try to tell anyone else about what you saw. Swear to me you won't go wandering off on your own looking for more *evidence.* If the perpetrators suspected they'd been seen, your lives could be . . ." She hesitated, unwilling to speak the unspeakable aloud. "Right now. Swear."

Fitz and Nelly stared at each other.

"But—"

"—Ma—"

Mrs. Dalton stood up to clear the table. "Then you may sing 'Happy Birthday' to me. The cake is not a total disaster. Fangs helped me to make it."

Theodore never got his cameo role in Episode Eight of *Clutch.* Thursday afternoon, when the studio cave was finally constructed, Henry walked the bear from the zoo to the stage. The two stood outside the dark, threatening entrance, Henry urging, Theodore obstinately balking.

"What now?" It had not been Holmquist's favorite week. The director was pulling at his thinning hair in frustration.

"He doesn't like caves anymore, Mr. Holmquist, sir."

Holmquist glanced at his hand, then wiped the hair grease distastefully on his trousers. "Ridiculous, Henry. Bears love caves. They sleep in them every winter."

"It's not near hibernation time yet. Theodore's still shedding."

"Remove him! Out of my sight!" Holmquist twirled. "Schmidt! Fetch a bear suit from the Costume Department. We might as well utilize your services now that you've finally chosen to grace us with your presence once more."

"The entrance to the cave!" Nelly screamed. "It's been blocked by an avalanche!"

"Good, Miss Dalton. Now spin around. What do you see?"

The camera was about a foot from Nelly's face, and in reality she couldn't see a thing aside from its single eye staring at her. However, she knew what she was supposed to see. "A bear! There's a huge bear coming at us from the back of the cave . . . and he looks *hungry*. We're trapped!" She swooned becomingly into Lieutenant Lloyd Wright's arms and relaxed there, congratulating herself on a rather neat piece of melodrama.

"Cut! Very good, all. Now let's reposition for the bear

shot." Holmquist fussed with his lens and turned to Sam. "Move the camera a few feet that way, I think. Lloyd? Here's where you suddenly discover you have a bear phobia . . . You may relinquish Miss Dalton for the moment, Lloyd. She's come out of her swoon. Think *bears,* Lloyd . . . Face-to-face with your own inner torments, you drop Miss Dalton and turn into a miserable, cowering shell of a man. That, of course, leaves young Dalton to rescue his sister once more." Holmquist stopped to rub his hands gleefully. "Young Dalton, however, has been busy trying to clear a path through the rubble, and by the time he gets to his sister, it's almost too late. Schmidt? Ready?"

Schmidt lumbered onto the cave set on his hind legs.

"No, no, Schmidt. On all fours, please, for the beginning of the shot. *Then* you rise to the occasion. Let's have some emoting here. You're famished"—the director grabbed Nelly's arm—"and before you is the most delectable of morsels—"

Schmidt growled out something from his snout that sounded like *schrek-lick* and fell on all fours to pad to the rear of the cave.

"Ready, Sam? Shoot!"

Schmidt emerged from his lair, rose to his hind legs, and staggered forward to grab for Nelly. Through the yellowed teeth of his mask, Nelly could smell cabbage and garlic. She held her breath while the bear began to hug her . . . and hug her . . . and hug her. Nelly steeled her body. It was only another scene, after all. A professional actress could deal with a little garlic. She tried to ignore the sharp pin of her father's badge suddenly piercing her skin, tried to let out her breath, tried to fight for more, but the hug continued. Black dots appeared before her eyes. A strange dizziness overcame her.

"Cut! You're a bear, Schmidt, not a boa constrictor! Let go!"

Nelly crumpled to the floor of the cave.

9
Buried Alive!

Fitzhugh Dalton brains the attacking bear with a rock, thereby saving his sister. Lieutenant Wright is still distraught, and it is Fitz and Nelly who must tunnel through the avalanche to safety. Supporting the lieutenant, they manage to find a road and beg a ride home. Surprised by their state, Paul Panther suggests a period of rest, but the intrepid twins resolve to procure a real clue to bolster their case before the Secret Service. They will continue their investigation—on the Jersey tidal flats themselves, where munitions are being shipped and are ripe for sabotage.

—"This Week at the Serials," *Moving Picture World*

"Why did you write in Black Tom, Mother? I'm not ready to go back there. I may never be ready to go back there."

"It's not specifically Black Tom, Nelly. Our feelings are mutual on that. It could be any dock in the area. Besides, this is the ninth episode, and I'm running out of inspiration."

It was another humid Saturday night, and the Daltons were halfheartedly talking in their kitchen-sitting room. Fitz was draped over a stuffed armchair, lethargically paging through the German dictionary. Nelly was on the rug, playing tug-of-war with Fangs. Dorothy Dalton was ensconced in the other upholstered chair, reading a magazine.

"Really." She looked up. "I cannot understand why *Harper's* sent back my article on the Suffrage Movement. Here's another one that's not nearly half as good."

"They probably accepted that one first, Mother," Nelly consoled her.

"Wait a minute!" Fitz's feet dropped to the floor. "I found *schrek-lick*. It's spelled almost like it sounds—*schreck-lich* . . . That stinker Schmidt."

"Spit it out, Fitz. We can hardly wait."

"Well, if that's how interested you are, Nell, maybe I'll just forget the whole thing. It was you he was insulting, after all."

"Please don't bicker, children. It's far too hot."

"Disgusting!"

"What was that, Fitzhugh?"

"That's what it means, Ma. *Disgusting!*"

Mrs. Dalton was not impressed. "If I had to walk around in a moth-eaten bear suit in this heat, I'd probably find it fairly disgusting, too."

"That was no reason for the clod to practically squeeze the life out of me."

"He said it was an accident, Sis. He said the forepaws of the suit unaccountably constricted him. He even apologized, and rather decently for him."

Fangs suddenly let go his end of the rag being contested, and Nelly tumbled onto her back. "Stop laughing, Fangs!" She turned to her brother. "And it didn't feel like any kind of an accident to me. That man is a menace."

"I don't know anymore, Sis. Look at it another way. He actually seems kind of lonely sometimes, living by himself and all. I think he keeps borrowing money from Panther just to have someone to talk to. I've even seen him pay it back. Maybe he's developed a kind of crush on you—"

That seemed to upset Mrs. Dalton more than the threat of violence. "A man in his thirties! That does it. I'm writing him out of the rest of the serial."

"It's too late. Cedric is impressed by Schmidt. All those bulging muscles."

"Really, daughter!"

"Well, Schmidt has got more muscles than Holmquist has—most of our director's are cluttering his brain. Dear Cedric would only write Schmidt back in again . . . like the liberties he took with the bear."

"Nell's right. We're stuck with Schmidt to the bitter end." Fitz let the German dictionary fall to the floor, then reached for the violin case propped next to the bookshelves behind him. He slowly loosened the catches and pulled out the instrument.

"Not even dusty." Fitz propped it under his chin and picked up the bow. The *skreek* that emanated sent Fangs into a howl. "Sorry, boy. It never sounded this flat when Dad played."

"That was not flat, Fitz, that was excruciating."

"True, Ma, but it was also excruciatingly flat." Fitz tightened up the strings and tried again.

Mrs. Dalton cringed. "Do put the violin away, Fitz. Until you choose to do your father honor by it."

Fitz languidly obeyed, then slung his long legs over the arm of his chair again. "Weekends were never this tedious when we lived in New York. There were the fellows from school to get together with, the occasional baseball game . . ."

"I wonder if Katy Cullan and Martha Goodkins got back from that camp in the Adirondacks yet?" Nelly thought aloud. "They were going to sleep in tents and everything. It sounded like fun."

"Maybe next Saturday we could take the ferry over and check out the old neighborhood, then catch a show or something."

"Leaving hearth and home to Fangs again? Sorry, Fitzhugh. That will have to keep until the autumn."

"Are you saying we're prisoners here, Ma? That we can't budge out of this apartment for the next six or seven weeks?"

"That's not at all what I said, Fitz. Although if you choose to interpret it that way . . ." She tossed aside her magazine. "Do you have any better ideas? Either of you? If it's a family democracy you want, I'm willing to talk. Heaven knows there's little else to do. We could add up all the mysterious accidents, then add up all our clues—"

"It's five to zero, in the bad guys' favor," Nelly piped up.

"How do you figure five to zero, Nell? I make it four–zero: the eavesdropper, the frog incident, the attack in the park, our burgled apartment—"

"I'm counting Schmidt's bear hug, Fitz."

"That's a non-event as far as I'm concerned."

"You weren't the one being hugged. And if you really want to be absolutely correct, it probably should be six–zero, counting the times Schmidt tried to shove us off the Palisades in that car chase—"

Mrs. Dalton's head jerked up from another magazine. "You never mentioned anything about that, either of you. And how you both can accept these things with such nonchalance, while I haven't had a decent night's sleep in days—"

Fitz swept his legs off the chair. "It's far too hot to think. How about some rummy, Sis?"

"I thought you'd never ask."

By Tuesday morning, all the Dalton mansion shots had been completed and another caravan left Pathmark Studios for the tidal flats of the great harbor of New York. Holmquist stopped its progress at an overlook to have Sam photograph background shots of freighters leaving for the war in Europe. Nelly and Fitz prowled around watching, while Holmquist slid into the military mien of General "Black Jack" Pershing, the hero of the day— legs planted wide, bearing straight, slapping a riding crop against puttees artfully wrapped up to his knees.

"Lafayette, we are coming!"

Fitz shook his head and edged away. The old boy was about to wax poetic. Holmquist performed on cue.

"The fruits of our labors and fields are being shipped to the needy across the sea. Bombs to destroy the enemy! Grain to nourish the survivors!" He stopped. "Say, that's not bad." The director shoved the crop under one arm to reach into a pocket for a small notebook and pencil stub. "It'll make a great introduction to the episode. How did that go?"

"Bombs to destroy . . ." Fitz offered.

Holmquist scribbled madly. Finished, he allowed his

eyes to scan the panorama once more. "And waiting, just waiting out of sight beyond the horizon—U-boats to annihilate all . . . Remember the *Lusitania*!"

Fitz and Nelly groaned in unison at the clichéd battle cry. Holmquist didn't notice. Buoyed by his creation, he cheerfully urged the caravan down to the flats.

"Is the tide supposed to be out?" Holmquist stood on the edge of a marsh about a quarter mile from the nearest munitions dock. They'd tried shooting there first, but had been chased off the premises in no uncertain terms for "security reasons."

"Yes, sir, Mr. Holmquist." Ernest the assistant nervously brushed lank hair out of his eyes, back over his careful center part. It immediately fell forward again, two wings framing his narrow forehead. "You specifically requested quicksand. I checked the tidal charts."

"So where is it?"

"The quicksand, sir?" A hand flicked up to the hair again.

"Of course the quicksand! Isn't that what we're standing in this muck discussing? The Dark Invader has cleverly lured our heroine over the treacherous sands by means of a series of clues. Clues suggesting, just suggesting, that there might remain shards from the devices that destroyed Black Tom so effectively. Miss Dalton is finally closing in on some real physical evidence. Or so she believes." The director chuckled with pleasure, for a moment truly believing his fiction. His chuckle died as he turned on Ernest again. "The quicksand?"

"Well, Mr. Holmquist, I didn't know you actually wanted to *use* it—"

"Dolt!"

Ernest flinched and backed off, as if expecting to be struck by Holmquist's riding crop. Nelly did note the crop twitch expectantly before falling idle by the director's side.

"It's probably out there about a hundred feet, isn't it, Ernest." She spoke with calm acceptance. New York's tidal flats weren't noted for quicksand, but with Holmquist's current record, it was bound to exist. Only seven more chapters to go, counting this one. Surely she could survive seven more chapters. "Where the little puddles in the sand are reflecting the sun."

"Why, yes, Miss Dalton. I'd judge that to be approximately correct."

"And when is the tide scheduled to return, Ernest?"

The young man squinted into the sun directly overhead. "I expected us to be here somewhat sooner, but those other stops took longer than I thought . . ."

"When, Ernest?" Nelly pushed.

"About an hour and a half, miss."

"Time's awasting!" roared Holmquist. "Have you got those planks to hold the camera steady over the sand, Sam? Good. Come along, Miss Dalton." He grabbed her arm and began tiptoeing over the damp sands. A sudden thought slowed him. "Somebody bring a shovel," he yelled over his shoulder. "If the quicksand isn't quick enough, we'll dig a hole."

Nelly struggled after the director, pausing only to glance back for her brother. He was grinning, the wretch.

All he had to do was pull her out of the quicksand, not be buried by it.

The sands did not, after all, swallow Nelly to Holmquist's aesthetic requirements. This was learned after she stood alone and expectant, etched against the bleak landscape, for well over fifteen minutes, waiting to be engulfed farther than her ankles. A hole had to be dug. Ernest philosophically began wielding the shovel.

"It doesn't seem that much damper down here, Mr. Holmquist. At least at the moment. But the tide does appear to be returning. Perhaps we could just bury Miss Dalton to the waist?"

Holmquist was rubbing his chin, watching the tide inexorably creep back. "All right, then," he grumbled. "Vacate, Ernest, and we'll set up the shot. Although why nature denies me the brilliance of an almost complete burial I cannot say."

Ernest squelched out and Nelly eased in, with a passing sigh for her frock. It was a becoming sea-green cotton, chosen with the day's adventures in mind. The sand and salt would do little for the Irish crochet trim. Yet another week in which the Dalton family's laundress made a fortune. When would picture studios take on the responsibility of completely costuming their actresses?

"It's cold!" she yelped as her bare feet touched bottom.

"Offer up your sufferings to the gods of cinematic art, Miss Dalton, and do let us get on with it."

Fitz was standing dry and comfortable on a piece of board between the director and the cameraman, waiting for his rescue scene. He watched as Ernest artistically sculpted sand around Nelly's waist. It really was quite evocative. Now settled about her, the grains seemed to be actually absorbing his sister. Holmquist, however, was yet unsatisfied. He strode off the safety of the planking to stand a couple of yards to one side of Nelly.

"It's not right! The sand ought to be creeping up on her, inch by inch, inexorably. What's required is the illusion that it's actually *sucking* at her. Sucking her down to a sticky, cloying, squelching death."

Fitz blinked. It must be one of Holmquist's illusions. Nelly was still solidly trapped to the waist, while the director's putteed legs were disappearing into the sands a scant six feet from his buried sister. Holmquist took no notice.

"Are icy tentacles grasping for you, Miss Dalton? No? Well, they should be. Icy tentacles slurping and swallowing hungrily."

The puttees were long since swallowed. The sands were past Holmquist's knees.

"Think *hollow* and *ravenous,* Miss Dalton. Think—"

"Good grief!" The sand was now up to the oblivious director's hips. Fitz turned to the cameraman, who was glued to his lens, chuckling. "Sam, we ought to do something!"

"Absolutely." Sam began to grind the camera. "Holmquist never did apologize properly for either the cave or the bear. Wait till the studio crew gets a load of this footage."

A magnificent slurp swallowed Holmquist to his waist. He finally noticed. "Quicksand! The real thing! It's sucking me into it!" He flicked his crop against the sand impotently, then peered beyond. "The tide! It's coming in! Help!"

Sam was still grinding and grinning. "Nonsense, Mr. Holmquist. We've got another half hour."

"But, but—"

With a belch of satisfaction, the sand rose to Holmquist's neck. "The rescue! Now! For heaven's sake, rescue me!"

Fitz hadn't waited for the order. He was already squelching over the lethal sands past his dumbfounded, half-buried sister. Arms outstretched, he neared the danger zone. "Hang on, Mr. Holmquist. I'm coming!"

The cameraman continued his steady crank as Fitz, now knee-deep, reached the director. Holmquist's shoulders were buried, and Fitz had to grasp at his head. That didn't work. Fitz grabbed for thinning hair. Holmquist screeched.

"For God's sake, don't pull it from the roots like that! Do you want me totally bald?"

An inch of water flowed around Holmquist's chin. He gasped, then shut his mouth. Fitz kept yanking with all of his might. The director rose half an inch.

"Mercy, Sam." Nelly had finally woken from her trance and began to burrow out of her own hole. "You've had your joke. Where's that shovel, Ernest?"

The camera stopped. Fitz's own legs began to be sucked under. "I'm losing him! Give me a hand before we're both buried alive!"

10
Wolf among Sheep

Saved from the quicksand and the sea by her heroic brother, Nelly finds herself more exhausted in spirit than in body from her most recent brush with death. She reluctantly agrees when her guardian recommends a sojourn in the country. Panther chooses a nearby farm that is coincidentally housing livestock soon to be shipped to the Allies.
—"This Week at the Serials," *Moving Picture World*

"After that quicksand business—" Nelly began, only to be stopped by her brother's sudden bellow of laughter. "What's so funny, Fitz?"

"The look on Holmquist's face after the rescue. Trying to salvage his precious dignity and the serial all at once."

"Well, it was clever of our director to think of cutting in my anguished face with your rescue of *him* during the final editing process."

"Anything to save his skin with the front office. He was more scared of telling Enoch Morris he'd blown an entire day's shooting than of having me pull out fistfuls of his hair."

"You needn't be that superior. Just because baldness doesn't run in our family—"

"Please, Nelly," Dorothy Dalton intervened. "What were you beginning to say?"

"Oh." Nelly remembered the script in her lap. "After the quicksand, this is the most gruesome episode yet, Mother. Inoculating poor dumb animals with germs—"

"Yes, it is quite diabolical," Mrs. Dalton complacently agreed with her daughter. "But it suddenly occurred to me to stop playing silly games with the screenplays. It is meant to be a propaganda piece, after all." She was perched on a wicker rocker on the front porch of their rooming house, fanning herself. "So then I thought, what's the worst a devious mind could conceive? And I came up with the anthrax germs."

Fitz and Fangs were both panting by her feet in the Sunday afternoon heat. "Anthrax wouldn't do a lot of good tossed into the water supply of a big city like New York, either," Fitz surmised.

Nelly shivered through the sweltering temperature from her seat on the porch railing. "That's past diabolical, Fitz. How could a rational human being even consider—"

"The Germans have been using poison gas in the trenches, Sis. It's in the papers every day. How far can they be from trying germ warfare?" He struggled to his feet. "I'm running upstairs for some cold water. Shall I bring a pitcher?"

Nelly blanched. "I may never drink water again!"

Fitz returned with a sparkling glass of the liquid and wafted it past his sister. "Innocent, colorless. Who knows what evils lurk within?" He downed the entire contents with gusto and set the empty glass on a porch step. "Ma may have a point. Bring the serial into the realm of the possible—which just happens to be almost as absurd as her fiction—stir it around a little, and . . ."

Mrs. Dalton frowned. "And what, Fitz? It was never my intention to precipitate another avalanche, or more muggings in the park . . . Oh, dear," she said with a sigh. "I wonder if it's too late to change the whole episode? If I run right upstairs to the typewriter—"

"Holmquist already approved Episode Ten when you brought it by on Friday afternoon, Mother," Nelly pointed out. "He said he was going to check on 'suitable pastoral environments' during his weekend drives into the country."

The fan started swaying in Mrs. Dalton's hand once more. "It seems as if wheels are already turning, then. Why is it always easier to begin something than to end it?"

It was marginally cooler in the countryside, and Fitz and Nelly spent two almost idyllic days there, posing for the camera with chickens and sheep, standing by wooden fences offering carrots to friendly horses and mules who bunched up for the privilege. It was only on Wednesday morning that things turned grim.

"You want me to, to do *what,* Mr. Holmquist?" Fitz almost stuttered in his dismay.

The director carefully realigned a beret over his recently depleted hair, then gave it an extra pat for security. "Ride a horse, young Dalton. Surely a simple request? Your sister, too, of course."

Nelly, for once, didn't mind. She'd been in love with the creatures for years, but their comfortable household before her father's death had not quite encompassed a pony. To finally mount one was the culmination of countless small-girl dreams. "You read the script, Fitz. You knew it included a chase scene on horseback."

"I never got past the germs last Sunday, Nell. I assumed we'd just catch the Dark Invader at his nefarious task by moonlight or something—"

"By moonlight?" Holmquist considered. "What a romantic idea! We'll shoot day-for-night. We haven't tried *that* yet. If Sam's got the proper lens filters with him, he can make broad daylight look like midnight. And we can have a nice blue tint added to the scene, too!"

He trotted off to consult with the cameraman, throwing back, "Your noble steeds await you in the barnyard."

Schmidt was already mounted, his blocky weight looking somehow appropriate atop a massive Clydesdale. Fitz blanched when he saw the size of the horses. His earliest childhood memory—he'd been barely three—was of his father's pulling him from the path of just such a carthorse moments before he would have been crushed beneath its hooves.

"No. They'll never get me onto one of those. It would be worse than tumbling off a cliff to fall from that height. Directly into the path of those legs, churning—"

A farmhand standing nearby ready to assist stroked an

animal. "This big guy's going across the water soon. Takes a great brute of a beast to lug a cannon, after all." Then he noted that Fitz was completely serious in his fear. "Don't worry, son. He may be big, but Clydes are gentle as lambs. Gentle and patient. It's a skittish Thoroughbred you should be scared of, and we've only a few of those boarding with us. The private mounts of some rich cavalry officers they are, waiting their turn for the big boat ride."

"Still and all . . ." Fitz gulped. He couldn't help being unreasonable. "Haven't you anything else smaller?"

Holmquist arrived in front of the barn to catch the last remark. He glanced up at Schmidt, then over to Fitz. "Perhaps you have a point, young man. Unwittingly, of course. If the force of wickedness was pursuing on a mount twice as big as the hero and heroine's, it would make their plight that much more effective . . . Not to mention emphasizing the immense, overwhelming nature of Evil itself." He paused. "Yes, I do like that. Symbolism. It almost makes a philosophical statement." He turned on the farmhand. "Fetch some smaller horses, my good man."

"But these are already saddled—"

"Is not Pathmark Studios paying you a healthy fee to keep me happy? Well, smaller horses will keep me happy."

Scratching his head, the man led away the first of the two waiting Clydesdales.

"Where did this new phobia come from, Fitz?" Nelly had been listening and wondering.

"You don't remember, Sis? Maybe you weren't with us

that day. Dad probably played it down, so as not to upset Mother—"

"What are you going on about?"

Fitz shook his head at her incomprehension. He knew it had happened. "Believe me. I'd rather face another cave filled with bears and Bengal tigers."

In due time, the substitute horses arrived. They were slim, sleek, powerful, and obviously—

"Thoroughbreds!" Fitz ran from the nearest with alacrity.

"Sorry, son," the farmhand announced. "These were the closest to hand. And they're overdue for exercise. Get real keyed up, do Thoroughbreds, without their regular exercise. Got totally different dispositions than a Clyde—"

The two fresh horses skittered on their reins, proving the point. Fitz remained ashen.

"Well, anyway, this bay is Yankee, and the chestnut is Dixie Do—"

Holmquist had had enough chitchat. "Let's get on with it. I want this scene shot before we have to return to Fort Lee later this afternoon."

Nelly was helped onto Dixie Do's back and sat there expectantly, feeling the power of the tensed muscles beneath her. Here at last was a situation she felt she could deal with. She bent forward to stroke the fine head. "Good boy, Dixie. This is going to be fun!"

Fitz, in his nervousness, approached the nearest side of Yankee and tentatively slung up a leg. The horse shied and Fitz slid onto the ground.

"Didn't know you was that much of a beginner, son. I

surely wouldn't recommend trying to mount from that
side again. Horses got a right side and a wrong side, just
like most people."

Fitz dusted himself off wordlessly and tried the correct
side. Yankee shook his head and pranced. Fitz clung
mightily.

"Also wouldn't recommend lettin' the horse know how
nervous you are. They sense it and kind of take advantage—"

The last words of wisdom came too late. Yankee had
bolted, straight out of the barnyard, toward the dirt road.

"Sam!" Holmquist yelled. "Start the car engines. The
chase is on!"

Nelly reached back to release her mass of golden hair. She
was fleeing by moonlight, after all. Her tresses should be
flowing behind her on the wind, reflecting moonbeams.
Pins were tossed to the road and her hand gripped the
reins again . . . This was being alive. This was what Fitz
must have felt like when he drove Holmquist's Packard.

Blithely ignoring body-jarring bounces, she took her
attention from the horse to glance quickly ahead. Fitz was
still in the lead, and apparently still hanging on to Yankee. She twisted her neck back. Schmidt was gaining like
the Furies.

It was all working out according to Mother's script.
Nelly was to be caught between Fitz and the Dark
Invader, having snatched a vial of lethal germs from the
villain before he could put his deadly plan into action.
Now the vial would be in her pocket, the ultimate evi-
dence for the Secret Service. Should the Invader catch her,

however . . . Nelly lurched at another bounce and clung more tightly . . . Worse even than being caught was the danger of falling from the galloping steed, crushing shards of the vial against her tender skin. There was no antidote for the toxin that lay within. Nelly grinned. She was taking the script a little too seriously.

Her eyes focused on the road ahead once more. At some point Fitz was scheduled to wheel around and confront Schmidt. How would he manage that? Her eyes widened. It was going to be an especially difficult feat. Fitz was no longer astride his mount.

Fitz struggled from the ditch into which Yankee had unceremoniously chucked him. He flexed his limbs. Stiff, but working. He tossed his head. Oof. That was a mistake. It must've gotten a solid crack in landing. Well, good riddance to the beast that'd thrown him, anyway. A battle-crazed horse was of little use to a determined cavalry officer.

Groggy, Fitz paused by the ditch. There was something yet to be done. What was it? Stop the Dark Invader. Yes, that was it. Fitz inspected his surroundings. How could a dismounted warrior stop a mounted one? His eyes rested on the loose pole of a nearby fence. Of course. Any medieval foot soldier worth his salt would have the solution in hand. Fitz grabbed for the pole and hefted its weight. This nonsense had to stop. A red-blooded American couldn't allow a saboteur to continue plying his trade in the Land of the Free.

Fitz strode to the middle of the dirt road. He found the balance point of the weapon as Nelly galloped by.

"Fitzzzz!"

Her cry drifted back to him. Fitz, unheeding, stood firm. The Devil's own helper bore down, his giant steed blowing smoke and fire from his nostrils. Would the monster stop? Or would Fitz be crushed? Childish fears must be cast aside for the greater need. He must act the man. His country's future lay in the balance, and the time for heroics was now.

The hooded villain reined in the galloping beast. Fitz watched it prance on hind legs. Excellent. The varlet was already cowed, and he, Fitzhugh, son of Dalton, was prepared. It would be done. He hefted his weapon, felt its weight, struck out. He reached his mark. The enemy was falling, was down. Vanquished forever. Fitzhugh Aloysius Dalton stood over the Dark Invader's prone body, brandishing the halberd in his hands.

The sound of manic cranking broke Fitz's concentration. He looked up.

"My God, what have you done?" Holmquist was standing in the chase vehicle, bereft of his beret, tearing at his remaining hair in earnest. "Have you murdered Schmidt?"

"Schmidt?" Fitz removed his foot from the chest of his enemy. "Where are your eyes, General? Can't you see? I've finally caught our nemesis. The Dark Invader! I should be proposed for the Congressional Medal of Honor!"

"Cut!"

Holmquist leaped over the side of the automobile and knelt in the dust next to Schmidt. "Are you alive, man? Speak, in the name of heaven!"

Schmidt groaned and gradually sat up, pulling the hood from his head. "The boy, he has gone mad. Mad!"

"Oh, good. You'll live." Holmquist stood up to brush the knees of his breeches. "Still and all, that was a fairly clever reinterpretation of the plot." He turned to Sam. "You did catch it all, didn't you? Marvelous. Now, how can we twist it slightly so that Schmidt escapes after all . . ."

Fitz was sprawled on the sitting room rug, an ice pack on his head. "I don't feel too good, Ma."

"Yes, dear, I can understand that." Mrs. Dalton hovered over him, worried. "You must have given yourself quite a knock when that horse threw you."

"Talk about getting into character," Nelly chimed in. "When I finally figured out how to turn Dixie around, there was Fitz, defending the middle of the road, roaring like some lunatic. Things like, 'Evil is annihilated forever! The world is safe for Democracy!' "

Dorothy Dalton bent to feel her son's head. "After ten weeks of solid wickedness, on camera and off, I suppose it could come to this. I don't think you have a temperature, darling. Perhaps a slight concussion. Just lie there for a while." She sank to her knees. "I assure you both, children: next week's episode will be considerably tamer."

11

The Eye of Evil

Believing he has vanquished the Dark Invader forever, Fitzhugh Dalton momentarily drops his guard, allowing the villain to remount his horse and escape. Nelly, however, still clings to the vial. It is returned to the Dalton mansion, where Nelly refuses to relinquish it. As Lieutenant Lloyd Wright agrees, the twins' guardian decides to summon the Secret Service himself.
—"This Week at the Serials," *Moving Picture World*

"How's your head this morning, dear?"

"Right as rain, Ma. There's nothing like two days off shooting and a weekend of total boredom to make me want to get out of bed on Monday. And I'm hungry again, too. Bring on the pancakes!"

Dorothy Dalton carefully distributed the stacks she'd prepared: one for Fitz, one for Nelly, one for Fangs, and one for herself. Fangs chose to eat his without syrup and was glancing up from his empty bowl hopefully before she'd settled in her chair.

"Forget it, Fangs. You're just going to have to learn to savor your food."

He licked his chops as if to point out that he had

savored it, then gave up and settled with his head between his forepaws. Mrs. Dalton turned her attention to the twins. "Nevertheless, Fitz, I want you to take it easy this week. You, too, Nelly."

"That shouldn't be hard, Mother, not with the namby-pamby plot you wrote. No horses, no car chases, no excitement whatsoever!"

"Kindly keep your criticism to yourself, Nelly. I racked my brains to devise precisely that effect. Also, you might recall that you were singing a different song just a few weeks ago. It seems to me that your brother is not the only one being overtaxed of late." Dorothy Dalton reached for the syrup and began to pour. "This non-stop excitement cannot but have a debilitating effect in the long run. What's to happen when you return to school in another month? How in the world will you settle down to your studies?"

"They will seem a little mundane, Ma," Fitz managed with a full mouth.

"Swallow first, Fitz. And before that chew properly, please." Mrs. Dalton sighed. "You see, even your eating habits are taking on a cliff-hanging pace."

Fitz swallowed. "It does grow on you after a while, this serial business. I've even gotten used to old Cedric. If we were to just continue, for say another year, think of all the loot we could stash away—"

"Never!"

"Well, maybe . . ."

Mrs. Dalton and her daughter had answered simultaneously.

"I was only surmising—"

"There'll be no more suppositions of that nature, young man." She turned to her daughter, whose "maybe" had been perhaps more unnerving. "Ever. This summer was only meant as a stopgap. To get us on our economic feet for the winter. You've both another future ahead of you. In the real world. Among normal people."

Fitz mumbled something to himself.

"What was that, Fitzhugh?"

"I only commented that I'm not sure what's normal in the real world anymore, either. When you think about it, the serial and our lives seem to be converging. What with our mysterious events over the summer right here at home—"

"Only four more weeks after this one," Nelly thought aloud. "Wouldn't it be nice if we could solve our personal mysteries as easily as Ma works out solutions for the serial?"

"Just gaze into my eyes, my dear. That's right." Paul Panther, disguised by wig, Vandyke beard, and spectacles, was slowly swinging his watch on a long fob before Nelly's face. "You are feeling quite relaxed. So relaxed, you might care to close your eyes."

Nelly closed her eyes. She was being hypnotized into revealing where she'd hidden the toxic vial. Panther was masquerading as a Secret Service agent, although she'd never visualized a Secret Service agent quite that way.

She imagined *her* Secret Service agent. He'd be a thoroughly grown-up Lloyd Wright: a mature but virile forty; tall, with broad shoulders; a thick, wavy head of hair; clean-shaven—and a look of true-blue patriotism and honesty shining like stars from his eyes. She opened her own eyes. Panther definitely didn't fit any part of that description. What he did look like was a devious escapee from some Viennese asylum.

"Cut! *Why* did you open your eyes, Miss Dalton? We are supposed to be hypnotized!"

"Three swings of that watch couldn't hypnotize an idiot, Mr. Holmquist. As you might recall, I'm meant to be at least a step above that. I should be seeing it as a pendulum, inexorably swinging closer and closer—"

"Stop! That's it!" Holmquist had dropped his megaphone and was hopping with excitement. " 'The Pit and the Pendulum'! Poe lives! We'll devise an imaginary scene—what is actually going on in your brain as the hypnotism takes effect. The giant pendulum swinging closer and closer. The nearer it comes, the sharper its edge appears. Razor-sharp. And in the background, the Dark Invader, hooded, pushing the blade ever nearer. Oh, my, oh, my . . . this is going to be brilliant. This is going to be a first! Wait till the critics see this episode! Move over, Mr. Griffith—Hollywood, here I come!"

Dorothy Dalton listened that evening as Nelly described Holmquist's intentions toward her script.

"Could you sue him or something, Mother? I mean, he's changed everything! Golly, who wants to hover underneath a giant, razor-sharp pendulum? It really would cut back on the possibilities of dramatic emoting, too. All I'll get to do is lie there, just when I'm developing a knack for expressive acting—"

"I'm afraid the script's out of my hands, Nelly. That's

the problem with writing for the movies. The author has no artistic control whatsoever. Besides, the pendulum will most certainly *not* be razor-sharp."

"That remains to be seen in the morning, Ma," Fitz commented. "Our beloved director is a stickler for detail."

"Perhaps Fangs and I should take a stroll over to the studio tomorrow—"

"You won't be able to use Fangs as support, Ma. You know he always waits for you right outside the main door. Won't even put his snout over the sill." Fitz patted the dog lovingly. "You're no dope, are you, boy?"

Fangs barked his agreement, then stretched up slowly to wander over to his empty bowl. After inspecting it, he gave Mrs. Dalton an accusing stare.

"Oh, all right. Maybe it is suppertime. I hope you like spaghetti."

Sam lay flat on his back on the studio floor the next morning, the heavy camera straddling his body. Fitz squatted next to him, staring up at the pendulum that had been constructed overnight.

"I wouldn't want *that* to fall on me."

"It's not as heavy as it looks, Fitz. The frame's cardboard and the pendulum's really just balsa wood. The whole movie business is illusion." Sam squinted through the lens of his tool. "Although Holmquist is going to owe me one. If he thinks it's easy to crank from this position . . . him and his screwball ideas . . . give me a little elbow room, Fitz." Sam adjusted the lens and grabbed the crank. "All set up there, Phil?"

A "yep" floated down.

"Give that thing a swing and begin lowering it."

Sam started to crank, chatting all the while. "That sister of yours is fairly game. Not sure I'd like to be under this pendulum without the camera protecting me. From her perspective, like I am now, it certainly looks like the real McCoy."

Nelly and Fitz had waited around all morning for Sam to finish his point-of-view shots. Holmquist hadn't been happy with the arc of the pendulum's swing. After many corrections, and lunch eaten outdoors under the sun, it was Nelly's turn. She took one look at Schmidt, hooded and waiting off camera for his reaction shots, shrugged to herself, and lay on the floor.

"Spread out a little more, Miss Dalton. That's right, skirt wide, arms hanging loose. You've no constraints, but you are metaphorically tied down by your listless mind. The Dark Invader has done this to you. He's reached your very will, sapped it. He's made you incapable of defending yourself."

Nelly grunted at Holmquist's instructions and arranged herself accordingly.

"Good, Miss Dalton. Now the pendulum begins to descend. Only your face will respond. It will mirror first your lethargy, then your growing terror as lethargy is overcome by incomprehension, and finally fear—"

Nelly focused on the pendulum. It was swinging slowly, methodically down. Nearer and nearer. It was big. The blade at the bottom must be almost a yard across, cut like a scythe, like a crescent moon. It glinted and sparkled like the moon, too. How had those clever special-effects people managed that? . . . It was only a yard from her face now, closing in. The sparkle was truly beginning to look more and more like the keen blade of an embedded knife.

"It's oppressively near, Miss Dalton. And just beyond, the Dark Invader awaits your submission, your capitulation, your confession. *Where* is the vial? React!"

"Never." She writhed impotently. "Never!" The pendulum inched closer, gleaming wickedly. Impossible. Her imagination was playing tricks on her again.

"But you *will* tell, Miss Dalton." This time the voice was Schmidt's, heavy and thick with excitement. "You will tell *all*!"

Not impossible. Now the pendulum was a mere two feet from her face, and Nelly knew without a doubt. Its edge *was* razor-sharp. Paralyzed by fear, she could do nothing but scream.

Fitz was the only one present who could interpret the true tenor of Nelly's screams. The pendulum only inches from her face, he lunged and caught the smooth sides of the device to his body, stopping its momentum.

"Cut! Mr. Dalton! Why have you interfered this time, may I ask? There had better be an excellent reason."

Fitz was examining the crescent of the pendulum. "You bet there is, Mr. Holmquist. This thing's been doctored, and I'm taking it right up to the office tower to show Mr. Morris."

"No. Wait! Morris has become completely paranoid after that avalanche business—some nonsense about going too far with our anti-German theme. He might shut down the serial. Let us examine this incident in the light of reason."

"Someone tried to hurt my sister, sir. That's all the reason I need!"

Sam was walking from behind his camera. "Let me have a look at that, Fitz. Everything was all right this morning." Sam reached for the crescent, then dropped it like a hot coal. He stared at the palm of his hand unbelievingly as it dripped a fine line of blood. He raised his head slowly. "The kid's not fooling. Anybody got a handkerchief?"

Nelly remained forgotten on the floor, an arm finally slung across her eyes in protection.

12
Adrift

Waking from her fiendishly induced nightmare with a new suspicion, Nelly Dalton suggests to her brother that their guardian, Panther, might be in league with the enemy. But why? They flee with the vial for New York. Panther finds them en route on the ferry, and they must jump ship with their precious burden.
— "This Week at the Serials," *Moving Picture World*

Dorothy Dalton stopped her halfhearted pecks at the typewriter, squinted at several lines of copy, and ripped out the sheet of paper. She crumpled it into a hard ball and flung it clear across the kitchen table into the sitting room area. Fangs caught the discard in one leap and obligingly returned it, tail a-wag.

"Thank you, Fangs. You're the only one who appreciates my writing lately."

"Did you get another rejection, Mother?"

"In this morning's mail, Nelly. It was a short story for *The Century.* I don't understand. Mine was just as sentimental as the other claptrap they publish—"

"What if you tried breaking a few barriers, Ma?" Fitz was washing up the Saturday luncheon dishes, glancing intermittently out the window, wondering if the threatening clouds just past the apple tree might betoken a storm to bring relief from the heat. "Add a little more realism." He glanced at his sister. "Like Schmidt during the pendulum scene."

"What do you mean, Fitz?"

"Yes, what about Schmidt during the pendulum scene?"

He turned to his mother. "Maybe Nelly didn't even hear him. She was rather caught up in her imminent doom." Fitz wiped his sweaty face on his rolled-up sleeves and lowered his voice dramatically. " 'You *will* tell *all*.' Old Schmidt was really entering into the spirit of things."

"It is what he's being paid for, Fitz."

Fitz stacked the last dish to dry and wandered past the table to slump into his favorite armchair. "Sure, Ma, but for some reason, Schmidt always seems to be in the thick of things . . . You sure you couldn't make out those faces at the top of the Palisades just before the avalanche, Nell?"

"They were way too far, Fitz. You know that. But Schmidt was off that day—"

"Right. And Schmidt's the only one who didn't come outside for lunch just before the blade appeared in the pendulum. Said it was too hot."

"It *was* too hot. I almost went back inside myself, but Paul Panther was breaking everybody up with his Charlie

Chaplin routine. It always amazes me that someone who seems so proper and serious could do comedy. And Lloyd—"

Lloyd had been pretty funny with that shawl draped over his uniform, playing the coy young lady to Paul's bumbling attentions. Fitz chuckled and leaned back for the violin case as a rumble of thunder shook the room. Fangs yipped and covered his ears with his paws. Fitz laughed outright. "Is it the thunder—or the violin? Don't worry, boy, it's not music I'm searching for this time."

Mrs. Dalton gave up on her typewriter and wandered over. "What are you looking for, Fitz?"

"I'm not sure." Suddenly serious, he pulled up the lid. "But something's not right here, either. Dad paid a lot of money for this instrument. It ought not sound like it's been—" It was in his lap now, and Fitz was tapping the polished wood thoughtfully. "Just something that's been going through my mind."

Nelly left the window she'd been staring out of to balance on her knees by his side. Fitz continued his tapping as the thunder moved closer. Then he began to pull at the edges of the body.

"Fitzhugh Dalton, if you ruin your father's instrument—"

"Not to worry, Ma. Only checking for loose glue. Dad taught me to respect his violin, just not how to make it sing." A thunderclap struck too close for comfort. In the suddenly darkened room, Fitz squinted at an *f*-shaped sound hole. His head slowly came up. "Anybody got tweezers? There's something wedged inside. Maybe a piece of paper."

"On my dresser, Nelly—"

"I'm on my way, Ma."

In a few short minutes the three Daltons were bent over the kitchen table studying the thick sheet of paper Fitz had unfolded. Mrs. Dalton was trying not to wring her hands. "It's his notes for the story he was going to give me. It has to be."

"Switch on the light, Sis. I'm having trouble reading this. It seems a little disconnected, as if Dad was trying to get it all down fast—"

Nelly jiggled the switch ineffectively. "The electricity's off!"

"Candles." Mrs. Dalton was rushing to a cabinet. "We'll light a candle."

Soon a small, weak glow lit the table. "Do keep that paper from the flame, Fitz. If it were to catch—"

"You're right, Ma." Fitz moved the sheet.

"I can't stand it anymore!" Nelly was doing a little dance of frustration. "What does it *say*, Fitz?"

Fitz slowly began to read out the words from the past.

> *"My undercover men have been bringing me strange stories, which may bear fruit. Some quick notes . . .*
> *—merchant submarine* Deutschmark: *free entry to American harbors. carrying contraband? agitating Irish nationalists?*
> *—hideout in Manhattan (15th Street?) run by German opera singer?"*

Fitz's eyebrows rose. "Why would these people have a hideout, Ma?"

"I'm not quite sure. Possibly a place of refuge where these people, these *terrorists,* could meet to make plans—"

"Just like in your script. Where the Dark Invader conceals himself." His eyes glanced down again. "Whoa. I don't believe it!"

"What, Fitz?" Nelly was shoving him. "Let me see, too!"

"*The Dark Invader!* He's down here! At least, that's what the writing looks like. The ink sort of runs out on the end of the word.

"*—Dark Invad . . . : Capt. von R.?*
—Laboratory for germs: where?
—Dr. W.S.: incendiary devices—cigars, coal,
  dumplings

"Dad's shopping list *was* about bombs, Ma!"

"Hurry up, Fitz! What else does your father say?"

"Just some final notes:

"*Check with Jim at Secret Service. Check German*
vessels impounded in harbor. Get Jim to screen
longshoremen. Too many accidents at sea. Tighten
security at Black Tom."

Fitz looked up. "That's all . . . Who do you suppose Jim is?"

"Was Dad involved with the Secret Service?" Nelly wondered.

Mrs. Dalton fell into a hard-backed kitchen chair. Somehow a handkerchief had found its way into her hand and she was brushing it liberally over her damp cheeks. "Two years. Two long years."

Nelly put her arms around her mother's shoulders. "It's all right, Ma. But Dad is still trying to tell us something . . . I think we'd better find this Jim."

Fitz's head rose from the paper. "Do you suppose there's a Secret Service office in New York?" He glanced out the window at the pouring rain. "Even if there is, there's nothing we can do about it today. And tomorrow's Sunday . . ."

Mrs. Dalton straightened her spine decisively. "I shall go into Manhattan myself on Monday. With your father's notes."

"We ought to be with you, Mother—"

"No, Nelly. Fangs will protect me. It might appear suspicious if you didn't show at the studio. But"—she paused to give each of her children a look of steel—"none of this must go beyond the three of us. Is that understood?"

Nelly had trouble concentrating on Monday. They were shooting down by the ferry. She kept waiting for her mother and Fangs to show up for their trip into the city. When they did, even Holmquist noticed.

"Ah, Mrs. Dalton? Come to watch the shooting?"

"You know I wouldn't want to interfere with your artistic endeavors, Mr. Holmquist. Fangs and I are just off for a little shopping."

"Indeed." Holmquist carefully kept his distance from

the animal. "I'm sure the river air will be enjoyed by both of you. It's a lovely day."

Pleasantries thus exchanged, Mrs. Dalton and the dog boarded the outgoing boat. Once over the gangplank, Fangs stuck his head beneath a railing and smiled at Fitz and Nelly; then he gave one sharp bark and concentrated his attention on protecting his mistress. As the ferry pulled away, Nelly watched Fangs carefully shepherd her mother from the railing to a less threatening space. Nelly breathed a prayer for her mother's success and returned to the remaining background shots.

In midafternoon, Nelly and Fitz got their own ride as the crew boarded the ferry to shoot the scenes in which Panther caught up with the twins, feigning nonchalance, but obviously itching to get his hands on the vial. They swept across the Hudson and back three times until Nelly began to feel seasick. Or maybe the queasy feeling was only worry over her mother.

"Fitz." She caught her brother's arm. "Don't you think Ma should be back by now?"

"Hush up about that and climb into this lifeboat. Holmquist is trying to decide whether we hit the river in the boat, or with life preservers."

"We're surely not going overboard here and now, for real—"

"Nah. They'll do the water scenes in that big tank back at Pathmark. But try and make climbing into a lifeboat look interesting and artistic." He glanced back at the director. "Or we may be spending the next four days getting waterlogged in that tank!"

Fitz and Nelly returned to an empty apartment that evening.

"Golly." Nelly walked around the kitchen. "It feels so, so—"

"Lifeless. Desolate." Fitz had his head in the icebox. "Even this is practically barren . . . Not a thing to eat."

"Is that all you ever think about, Fitz? Food? I've been worrying my head off all day about Mother, while you—"

"Simmer down." He inspected the icebox and its meager contents once more. "Of course I'm worried about Ma, but worry gets you nowhere. Me, I'm a man of action, and action is currently called for. No food, no strength to get the bad guys . . . We could probably manage bacon and fried eggs. You want to toss for who cooks?" Fitz found a penny in his knickerbockers and held it poised in his fingers.

"All right," Nelly conceded. "Heads cooks, tails cleans up."

In a moment Fitz was cheerfully sawing away at a slab of bacon.

Dorothy Dalton and Fangs returned after nine. Nelly flew at them. "Where have you been? We've been so worried—"

"Ah, so the shoe finally slips to the other foot." Mrs. Dalton sank into an armchair. "Speaking of which, shoes first." She removed hers and sighed with bliss as she stretched her toes. "Fangs and I had something of a wild-goose chase. It wasn't till almost five that we finally found the lair of the Secret Service. Not very prepossessing, I must say."

"What about this Jim person, Ma?"

"That mystery, at least, is solved, Fitz. It would be a certain James Quinlan. But he was off in Washington and won't be back till next week."

"Did you talk to anyone else, Mother?"

"Quite frankly, Nelly, no one else seemed particularly interested. I believe they took me for a crank. One agent even attempted to remove Fangs from the premises and nearly lost his leg for his efforts." She bent down to pat the dog fondly. "I didn't like that one's looks anyway."

"What's the bottom line, Ma?"

"The bottom line, Fitz, is that I left an urgent message for this Quinlan. And that Fangs and I are both very hungry. I hope you saved some of that bacon I smell for us." She shrugged off her suit jacket. "Not an altogether successful day. I hope yours was better."

Nelly's climb into the ferry's lifeboat had apparently not met Holmquist's artistic standards. Tuesday found the twins floating in doughnut-shaped life preservers around the studio's water tank. Wednesday found them equally adrift. By Thursday, Nelly knew she'd be prematurely wrinkled for the rest of her life. That's when Holmquist brought in the fog machine, not to mention the foghorn.

Their director was delighted with his new toys—particularly the foghorn. He had it set to blast every thirty seconds. Each time it sounded off, Nelly nearly leaped out of her shriveled skin and her preserver. It created the distinct illusion that a freighter was about to run down the twins. Either that, or they were on the verge of being ground against jagged rocks, leaving nothing but bloodied pulp. Finally she could stand it no longer.

"Mr. Holmquist!"

"Yes, Miss Dalton?"

Nelly floundered within her preserver, bouncing her toes off the bottom of the tank. "I fail to see the necessity of the foghorn, Mr. Holmquist. We are shooting a *silent* film. The audience will never *know* about the foghorn."

"Ah, but *we* know, Miss Dalton. Don't we? And does it not add a little frisson of dread to your spine?"

"My spine has been paralyzed for hours, Mr. Holmquist. It couldn't feel a thing. But if that sick bull sounds off one more time, I quit!"

"Nelly!" hissed Fitz.

"I mean it, Fitz. It's giving me the most dreadful headache."

Holmquist sighed deeply from behind the lights. "Very well, Miss Dalton. It shall cease and desist. Ernest has to return it to the Lighthouse Service by evening anyway." He shouted to the fog maker. "More enthusiasm with that machine, Phil. I want a fog the consistency of pea soup. A London fog. Victorian. Dangerous. Capable of hiding Jack the Ripper—or worse, the Dark Invader himself!"

Fog rolled over the twins, thick and moist. Nelly choked and gagged.

"Excellent, Miss Dalton. You've been adrift for three days, floating out to the open sea. No food. No fresh water to ease your parched throat. The elements are conspiring against you. You're about to lose hope. *Nothing* can save you now . . ."

"Except a submarine," Fitz muttered.

"What was that, Mr. Dalton?"

"We're too low in the water, and the fog is shrouding us. Only a submarine could find us—"

"Why not, Mr. Dalton? Why not! Wave machine, please? I want some action! A storm is coming, and the Dark Invader is still searching for our heroes. He needs that vial!"

Nelly gasped as a wave hit her full in the face.

"Yes, yes. Respond, Miss Dalton! You see a light. A ship, perhaps? You're almost over your ordeal! Help is on the way. But will it be the right help?"

13
Bombs Bursting in Air

As the conning tower of a German submarine looms toward the exhausted, drifting twins like a hungry shark, another vessel heaves through the fog. On the verge of being shanghaied, the Daltons are rescued by Lieutenant Lloyd Wright of the U.S. Navy. They steam back to port, vial intact. The Dark Invader realizes his days may be numbered if he does not succeed at last. He returns to his secret laboratory to construct enough bombs to blow up the entire Dalton Estate.
—"This Week at the Serials," *Moving Picture World*

By Sunday evening, all three Daltons were frustrated.

"Do you think this Jim will actually get your message, Ma?"

"And if he does, can he be trusted to help?"

"I don't know, children." They were strolling back from an ice-cream parlor, licking at dripping cones. "But your father seemed to trust him."

They rounded the corner by the park and slowly made their way home. Just before reaching the house, Fangs began to bark and pull at his leash. His unexpected agitation made Nelly drop both the leash and her cone. Pausing only to lap up the scoop, Fangs barreled ahead.

"Fangs! How could you? That was tutti-frutti! My favorite!"

Mrs. Dalton sighed. "We could always walk back for another, Nelly. As soon as we collect—" She stopped to watch Fangs pant up the front steps of the big white house, where he leaped at a stranger peacefully rocking in her usual chair.

"Fangs! Down!" Nelly forgot her tutti-frutti. She was petrified. In another moment the porch might be covered with blood.

"He's no bother." The stranger stood up. "I've always liked a big dog." He ruffled the German Shepherd's fur and ambled to the top step. "You must be Mike Dalton's family."

Nelly didn't hear another word. Before her stood someone a mature but virile forty; tall, with broad shoulders; a thick, wavy head of hair; clean-shaven—and a look of true-blue patriotism and honesty shining like stars from his eyes.

"Nelly. Nell—"

Nelly snapped out of her trance. "What is it, Fitz?"

"You could at least shake hands with Mr. Quinlan of the Secret Service."

Monday morning, Cedric Holmquist was feeling patriotic, too. He sported a red, white, and blue scarf knotted under the open neck of a military-style blouse.

"It'll be just like the Fourth of July," he chattered happily. "Fireworks everywhere! Oh, it's going to be *such* fun blowing up the Dalton Estate!"

"But it's not actually meant to be blown up, is it, Mr.

Holmquist? I mean, Fitz and I are supposed to stop the
Dark Invader before he sets off his charges—"

"A mere trifle, Miss Dalton. He'll manage at least the
outlying explosions, and we'll have a sky full of wonder and
glory." Holmquist turned to an assistant. "You have talked
to the Vercelli Fireworks Factory about setting up their
wares in time for a Thursday night shoot, haven't you?"

Fitz rolled his eyes at Nelly. "Good try at keeping a little verisimilitude in Ma's script, Sis. But I think we're
getting fireworks."

"As long as we don't get caught in the middle of them.
Real fireworks can be just as dangerous as explosives.
Surely you haven't forgotten the standard lecture Dad
always gave us on the Fourth of July?"

"Right, while the other children were running all over
the block shooting off their firecrackers. Just once, I
wanted to do that!"

"You still have all your fingers, don't you? Not like
Tommy Upton—" Nelly stopped at her brother's expression. "And besides, Mr. Quinlan was supposed to come
back Thursday night to give us a progress report. Now
we'll miss that!"

"Maybe it's for the best. Ma deserves a little privacy."

Nelly's hand flew to her mouth. "You don't suppose—"

"I'm not supposing anything. But they did get along
well and—"

"—and Mr. Quinlan said how cozy our apartment was,
and how he missed having a real home and hearth."

"He's not married, Sis. And he took us seriously. The
whole story, from the beginning of the summer."

"It was nice being able to tell someone else. To get it off our shoulders and onto such strong ones."

Fitz yawned. "Yes, till midnight. I'm still bushed."

"Daltons!"

"Mr. Holmquist?"

"Out to the studio golf course. Golf is the perfect anodyne for almost being lost at sea."

"If you say so, Mr. Holmquist."

They played golf with Lloyd Wright for several days, in between arranging shots of a hooded Schmidt scurrying behind trees edging the course, villainously arranging his explosive charges.

Nelly felt she was truly getting the hang of the game at last. It was all a matter of attitude. If, instead of simply aiming at a little hard, white ball, one were to suppose it was the head of the Dark Invader—or even Schmidt . . . well, it added enormously to an otherwise silly enterprise.

Fitz marked his sister's growing prowess with amusement. "You really whomped that last ball, Nell. Why the sudden enthusiasm?"

"Merely a proper outlook, Fitz. Watch." Nelly bent over another ball, silently dedicated this one to Schmidt, and swung.

"Wow! Clear over the green! But you got yourself into a trap, Sis. It's going to be lost in the woods."

"Nonsense. Just wait."

The ball descended into the trees and a sudden yowl broke the afternoon air. It was followed by Schmidt, staggering out of the woods, ball in one hand, head clutched by the other.

"See?" Nelly smiled sweetly at her brother. "I told you it wouldn't be lost."

"Cut!" barked Holmquist through his megaphone. "I think we have enough golf shots."

Thursday night finally arrived. Fitz and Nelly ran home to swallow a quick dinner and were amazed to find another chicken roasting in the oven, the typewriter nowhere in sight, and their mother dressed in a freshly pressed summer frock.

Fitz gave her a quick kiss on the cheek. "You look great, Ma. But I didn't know you'd invited Jim to dinner."

"Mr. Quinlan to you, young man. And I didn't. I just thought he might be hungry after a hard day."

"Well, I am, too. Do we get some of that bird, or is it all for him?"

"Fitzhugh Dalton! Don't be so greedy!"

"It's all right, Mother," Nelly intervened. "He really is hungry. Me too. It's been a long day already, and we'll need extra energy to work late tonight."

"It's a very large bird, children. Sit."

Fitz gulped down his dinner, and the twins departed for the studio before the Secret Service agent arrived. They left their mother alone with Fangs and the cooling, decimated chicken.

Holmquist was pacing around the small golf course, casting frowns at the darkening sky. "It isn't going to storm, is it? Or be overcast? The fireworks would be ruined."

Fitz studied the pristine heavens yet again. "Not a cloud in sight, Mr. Holmquist. You picked a perfect evening."

"One never knows about these things, young Dalton. I did somewhat overshoot my budget on the arrangements. Without precisely obtaining permission from the office tower . . ."

Nelly actually felt a twinge of pity for the director. He wanted so badly to succeed. "They'll be delirious when they see the rushes, Mr. Holmquist. All will be forgiven."

Holmquist stopped pacing to stare at her. "Thank you, Miss Dalton. That was considerate. Of course the shots will work . . . Sam! Sam! Did you line up the extra cameramen?"

Full darkness descended. Nelly and Fitz were instructed to rush from the mansion to confront havoc surrounding them on all sides. Behind the false front of the house they waited for the first booming sounds, then bolted forth, to stop in amazement and horror.

There were fireworks, yes—great bursts of colorful shooting stars reaching to the heavens everywhere. But there was also fire. Real fire, from apparently real incendiary bombs.

Fitz jumped as two more bombs exploded in tandem dangerously close to the wooden façade of their mansion. Intense flames breached the night. "This wasn't in the script, Nelly."

Nelly's eyes were frozen on the scene in fascination and dread. "No, Fitz. It wasn't."

Jim Quinlan arrived before the fire engines.

"Fitz. Nelly. Are you all right?"

"Sure. But where's Mother?"

"She's coming with Fangs. I ran ahead." The agent quickly surveyed the chaos burning out of control around him, took in the last few whistles and pops of the dying pyrotechnics display. "If they're not careful, they might lose the studio building. The fire is getting too near . . . What happened? From your front porch it sounded like a war starting."

Nelly spread her arms. "Mr. Holmquist, our director, wanted fireworks—"

"—but someone else, it's becoming obvious, intended the real thing," Fitz concluded.

Quinlan ran fingers through his thick black hair as dark shapes hysterically raced around the area. "More sabotage, only the ante has been upped since that avalanche you described for me. We could attempt to organize the chaos . . . or we could try to get to the bottom of it. Before the evidence is gone."

"I'd go for the evidence, sir. There might not be another chance."

"Right, Fitz. You come with me. Nelly, wait for your mother—"

"Why? I deserve to hunt for evidence just as much as Fitz—"

"Nelly." Quinlan touched her arm. "I'm not trying to hold you back, but your mother needs to be reassured of your safety. You should be able to understand that."

"Yes, Mr. Quinlan." That it came out rather grudgingly no one noticed. Quinlan finished his orders.

"After that, see if anyone's been hurt . . . Do what you
can." The agent disappeared with Fitz.

Nelly was trying to spy out Holmquist and the cameramen when a large, furry body leaped into her arms.
"Fangs! And Mother!"

"Are you all right, darling? And your brother?"

"Not a scratch, Ma, either of us. Fitz went off with Mr.
Quinlan searching for clues. We've been ordered to give
succor to the needy."

Mrs. Dalton took in the scene as fire engines finally
began to arrive. "That might be a tall order. We'd better
begin."

It was a piece of unexpected clumsiness on Fitz's part that
did it. They'd been skirting several of the still-blazing
craters in the golf course behind the studio, half-blinded
between pitch blackness and raging flames.

"Oow!" He clutched at a foot and hopped a pace or
two.

"What is it?"

"I don't know, Mr. Quinlan. Something hard, like a
pipe, maybe, where it shouldn't have been."

"Don't move." Quinlan backed up and began pacing
the area. "Hah!"

Fitz hobbled over. Quinlan was gingerly examining a
thick metal object, rather like a very large Havana cigar.

"Stand back! It hasn't detonated as scheduled. That
doesn't mean it won't."

Fitz moved briskly, his eyes never leaving the device.

"It looks awfully close to what Dad was talking about. The cigars—"

"Precisely. Pathmark Studios seems to be harboring a very serious saboteur."

Nelly and Mrs. Dalton finally found Holmquist. He was sitting squat in the middle of the gravel drive in front of the studio building, watching firemen douse the wooden walls with water. His hair and clothing were scorched, his eyes glazed.

"Mr. Holmquist?" Nelly tried.

"I'll never get to California now," he mourned. "Never. Not once word of this gets out. Anathema. That's what my name will be."

"It's not your fault, Mr. Holmquist. *You* didn't set the real bombs. Only fireworks. And the footage is going to be lovely. Sam and his men are still shooting. We saw them."

The director looked up at Nelly blankly. "They are?"

"Yes! Besides the footage for Episode Thirteen, there'll be lots left over for the newsreels—"

His head twisted back to the studio. "If the main building doesn't catch fire. If it's saved . . . maybe I'll be, too. *In the Kaiser's Clutch* can continue . . ."

"Certainly, Cedric." Mrs. Dalton patted his shoulder. "Why don't you get up and check on Sam. To make sure he's getting the proper angles."

"Of course. The director knows best. The director must always remain in charge . . ."

Nelly and her mother shook their heads as Holmquist wandered off, swaying slightly from shock.

"Who shall we save next, Mother?"

"I'm not sure."

Fangs took the decision out of their hands by lunging suddenly against his leash, fur on end, a deep growl in his throat.

"What is it, boy?"

The dog didn't explain, only jerked from Nelly's grasp to plunge off into the darkness. In a moment a shrill human scream broke above every other sound. Nelly and her mother dashed toward it. So did everyone else in the area. Nelly bumped into Fitz in the crowd surrounding the outraged dog. They both stared at Fangs's victim with dawning comprehension.

"Shall we call Fangs off, Sis?"

"Why? The villain finally seems to be getting his just rewards."

Quinlan pushed through the horde. "Fangs! Down! Guard!"

Fangs removed his teeth from a thigh, but remained straddling the petrified man, teeth bared. Quinlan searched the victim. From a rear pocket he pulled out a long, thick cigar—a perfect duplicate of the one recently found on the golf course. Quinlan raised his head.

"Any idea who this is, kids?"

"Schmidt!"

"—or the Dark Invader?"

14

Laboratory of Doom

The Dark Invader's nefarious scheme to destroy the Dalton
Estate creates chaos, but little permanent damage. He
escapes once more, but leaves incriminating evidence,
which the stalwart twins find. Finally they have a clue to
his hideout, and full intentions of locating it at last.
—"This Week at the Serials," *Moving Picture World*

Jim Quinlan had typing paper spread all over the Daltons' kitchen table. He was covering the sheets with diagrams.

"The device is fiendishly clever." He pointed a pencil
stub at a drawing. "The cigar consists of a long tube of
lead. It's divided inside into two compartments by a copper disk." He glanced up. "The lab analyzed the liquids
in those compartments—"

"What were they, Mr. Quinlan? And could I make
something like this in chem lab at school?"

"Jim, please." Quinlan smiled. "We're in this together
now, after all . . . On one side picric—"

"Stop right there, Jim!" Dorothy Dalton's voice was

adamant. "I won't have Fitz getting any ideas about wrecking his scholastic career!"

"Aw, Ma. *I'm* not trying to blow up anything—"

Nelly poked her brother to hush him. "What happens next, Jim?"

Quinlan grinned at her. "Next, the open ends are plugged with wax. The two . . . substances . . . begin to eat through the copper . . . When they meet: *boom!* Sudden, intense flame. Perfect for starting fires in munitions plants, on ships—and in motion picture studios brave enough to be making anti-German propaganda films."

He ruffled his hair absently. "And here's the true beauty of the whole thing: after the incendiary bomb explodes, the lead casing melts completely. Not a trace is left. Small wonder we've had so much trouble catching these saboteurs."

"But how did Schmidt control the timing, Jim?" Now it was Dorothy Dalton asking the question.

"Timing depends on the thickness of the copper strip, Dory. One of these little babies could hide innocently in the hold of a ship for weeks, till suddenly—total havoc!"

The agent reached down to pat Fangs, whose head was lodged trustfully in his lap. "Somebody out there has got it down to a science, though—and I don't think the mastermind is our Mr. Schmidt. After almost five days of interrogation we've learned that he's thick-headed, all right—pure muscle and few brains."

Nelly pulled away from the diagrams. "So the Dark Invader is still out there somewhere."

"I'm afraid so, Nelly."

By the middle of the week, Pathmark Studios was once again functioning at full speed. Holmquist was back to normal, too.

"We're way behind on our shooting schedule, troops. I can fill in most of the background scenes for Episode Fourteen from unused footage, but the laboratory scene is new. Let's put our hearts into it!"

Fitz inspected the set in question. It had been quickly cobbled together from bits and pieces of old Pathmark pictures. It looked like nothing so much as his high-school science lab gone berserk. Bubbling vats, giant beakers, gadgets, gauges, and knobs were strewn pell-mell over tables and floor. "Hey, Nell—isn't this kind of fun? Look at that green stuff oozing!"

But Nelly was more interested in examining the secret sliding door that had been constructed in the library set adjacent to the laboratory.

"This is neat, Fitz. The hidden entrance to the Dark Invader's lab. You just press on one of these books . . ." She paused to read the title. "*Crime and Punishment.* You give Dostoevsky a little shove, and *voilà!*"

"Yeah, real cute, Sis." Fitz had already turned back to the lab. A career in chemistry seemed more promising all the time.

"Miss Dalton!"

Nelly jumped away from the secret door, mid-slide. Her frock was caught as it clicked shut. "Yes, Mr. Holmquist?" She tugged at her jammed hem.

"Please cease and desist toying with the props. I need you in the laboratory, directly next to the seething vat. The Dark Invader has you in his clutches once more and

is about to immerse you in acid. The perfect resolution
for such a bothersome heroine. No fuss, no muss. Total
dissolution into nothingness . . . Oh, dear, I do wish
Schmidt hadn't inconvenienced us so by getting himself
caught. He could at least have waited for the conclusion
of the serial!"

Nelly was reaching behind her frantically, blindly bat-
ting at books. She finally hit the key volume, the door
slid open with a hiss, and she was free. "I think our Ernest
will make a lovely Dark Invader, Mr. Holmquist." She
ran from the door before it entrapped her again.

"His build is all wrong!"

"Just pad out his shoulders a little, and maybe his
stomach, too—"

Holmquist clutched at his head dramatically. "Why
must people involve themselves in tawdry politics? Art
should rise above all that. Schmidt's nonsense has definitely muddled my masterpiece!"

Jim Quinlan was sitting on the front porch next to
Dorothy Dalton when the twins got home from the studio on Wednesday evening. Fangs was positioned strategically between the two. He barely even acknowledged
Nelly, just thumped his tail.

Nelly bent down to pet him anyway. "Switching soul
mates, Fangs? Hello, Ma, Jim. How's the plot working
out?"

"Which plot, dear? The final episode of *Clutch,* or the
saga of the saboteurs?"

Fitz sprawled on the steps. "We already know how
Clutch has to end. The Dark Invader is unmasked by

Nelly and me at last, saving America from the Kaiser's long grasp." He pounded on an imaginary instrument in front of him. "And the piano player launches into 'The Star-Spangled Banner.' "

Quinlan stirred regretfully in his chair. "I wish the real business could be solved as neatly, Fitz. Unfortunately, it can't." He rose to stretch. "I only stopped by for a few minutes to check how you were doing. I'm due back at the office for night duty with our friend Schmidt. He still hasn't cracked, hasn't given us one name! Schmidt won't even say why he was terrorizing you people. I don't know . . ." The agent stood, unwilling to leave.

"You're sure you can't stay for dinner, Jim?"

"Sorry, Dory. But I plan to make it up to all of you." He brightened. "How about Saturday night? I'll be off work. Let me treat you to dinner in the city. Lüchow's."

Fitz's eyebrows rose. "A German restaurant?"

"Have you ever tasted Lüchow's Wiener schnitzel, Fitz? Or their sauerbraten?"

Fitz shook his head dumbly.

"Enough said." Quinlan made a little bow. "Until Saturday, then. I'll meet you at the restaurant at seven."

The remainder of the week passed slowly. At the studio, no matter how Holmquist begged and cajoled, his cast's heart was not truly in the final episodes of his masterwork. Ernest may have been good with quicksand and tidal charts, but he made a pitiful villain. Even hooded, he emanated none of the tight fury that Schmidt had had.

"Ernest." Holmquist was pulling again at the hairs slowly regrowing on his head. "*Try* to convey some men-

ace. Only *try*! The young lady who has foiled each and
every one of your plans . . . the weak, helpless female who
may become responsible for the end of your brilliant
career as a master spy—she's in your hands! Grab her!
Hoist her up! Shove her toward the acid vat!"

"It's not a very nice thing to do, Mr. Holmquist, sir."

"Of course it's not a very nice thing to do! You are not
a nice person! Archvillains are not nice people, Ernest.
But pretend. Please?"

Somehow Ernest managed to grab Nelly, managed to
hoist her toward the vat. Somehow Fitz stormed in and
saved her again. The scene was shot only once. Holmquist
studied his actors.

"No retakes, Sam. We'll just have to live with the
scene as it stands. It's Friday afternoon. Go home, everybody. Rest. But you'd all better be feeling appropriately
malicious by Monday!"

Schmidt safely incarcerated, the Daltons felt fairly secure
in leaving Fangs home on Saturday. With light hearts
they boarded the ferry for New York and took a trolley
to Manhattan's Lower East Side to meet Jim Quinlan.
They found Lüchow's on Fourteenth Street in the old
German district.

Mrs. Dalton entered the establishment with some
trepidation. "I'm not certain ostentatious gastronomy is
quite my style, children." She nervously touched a ruby
earring, finally reclaimed for the occasion. "Particularly of
the heavy German sort . . ."

Fitz registered the ornate interior and whistled softly.
"Would you look at all those crystal chandeliers, and

enough potted palms to decorate an entire South Seas island! I'm glad Jim is treating. This looks like a week's salary for sure."

"Hush, Fitz." Nelly nudged him. "There he is."

Jim Quinlan strolled over and took Mrs. Dalton's arm. "I'm so pleased you could come. I almost feared—"

The headwaiter bustled over. "Your reserved table is ready, Mr. Quinlan. And the Liebfraumilch you ordered is chilling."

"Thank you, Dieter."

This time Fitz poked Nelly. "They're treating Jim just like a big shot. How's that for service?"

"Ssh!" Nelly smoothed her skirt, raised her head high, and made believe she truly belonged in the place as they swept to their table.

Some time later, Fitz sagged back in his chair, stuffed beyond gluttony. He'd never be able to rise from this table. Never move again. Idly he let his eyes roam over the crowded dining room, let them drift like the surrounding smoke from after-dinner cigars. They stopped on a familiar figure.

"Jim!" His languor gone, Fitz was sitting bolt upright.

"What is it, Fitz?"

"Behind you, four or five tables back. It's Panther, with a bunch of very German-looking men!"

"Who's Panther?"

Nelly was twisting her head. "Paul Panther, our guardian from *In the Kaiser's Clutch*. He's been awfully sweet to us. Maybe we should go over and say hello."

"Funny, but suddenly I'm not so sure about that, Sis. I

don't like the looks of those people he's with . . . And it just came back to me—"

"What?"

"He was absent from shooting the day of the avalanche. Don't forget there was more than one person wrestling with that boulder!"

"I really believe you're letting your imagination run away with you, Fitzhugh. Mr. Panther has been the soul of charm and civility—"

"Turn around, Dory, Nelly. No more staring, please." Jim raised his hand to beckon for the check. "Fitz, keep an eye on that table discreetly. When they seem ready to leave, tell me. Lesson number one of any police work: never ignore coincidence . . . Everyone finished?"

"I've still got half my Black Forest cake, Jim. I was trying to take my time—"

"It's now or never, Nelly."

Nelly forced down another gooey bite.

Panther and his party walked slowly down the street, so deeply engrossed in their conversation that they never noticed the four people trying to trail them inconspicuously a half block behind. Voices drifted back, the sound if not the content.

"They're speaking German, Jim!"

"I noticed, Fitz."

"Mr. Panther never let on he could speak German," Nelly observed. "Not in the entire last fourteen weeks at the studio."

"Another interesting point," Quinlan commented placidly as he strolled arm in arm with Mrs. Dalton.

Panther's group turned at the next corner, continued on a block, then disappeared into a brownstone town house halfway down West Fifteenth Street. Quinlan held the Daltons back at the corner. "Fifteenth Street. We're no longer talking coincidence, Dory. This is too close to the notes you found of Mike's. Can you get yourselves safely back to the ferry? I hate to abandon you, but the situation needs to be explored."

"Not without me!" Fitz was vehement.

"Or me!" Nelly was equally so.

"There is no way I will have any of you endangered. These could be treacherous people—"

Fitz stood firm. "Just what do you think we've been involved with all summer, Jim? I think we deserve to be in at the conclusion of this business. It was our father and Black Tom that started it, after all."

"My brother is right," Nelly agreed.

The agent looked to Mrs. Dalton. "I'm afraid I haven't any help I can call in on a Saturday night. The Bomb Squad is off duty weekends."

"That's outrageous, Jim!"

"It's all funding. President Wilson is too much of a gentleman to believe in foreign spies. Sometimes I'm sure the Germans are taking this War much more seriously than we are."

Dorothy Dalton stood torn between her children's safety, their valid complaints, and her desire to have the affair ended for once and all. She spread her arms. "Perhaps if we were all to knock on the door, ask for the Brown family or something—"

"Too obvious." Quinlan was pacing around the Daltons. "As soon as Panther—if he's truly involved—as soon as he spots the twins, it will be all up."

"What about investigating from the cellar?" Fitz suggested. "There must be a coal chute or something—"

The Secret Service agent stopped in mid-stride. "It's better than nothing. But I mean what I said. This part of the job is mine. I insist you all go home and leave me to it."

Dorothy Dalton gathered the twins and pointed them in the direction of Fourteenth Street. "He's absolutely right. We'll just splurge on a cab to the ferry and—"

Fitz's head was twisted back, watching Quinlan's already disappearing figure. He stalled till the agent was out of sight, then made a mad dash into the darkened street.

"Fitzhugh Dalton!"

Nelly chose that moment to pull her arm from her mother's. Enough of this nonsense. If Panther had truly been behind Schmidt's activities, *he* was the one ultimately responsible for getting her attacked in the park, stomped on in the marsh, and almost shredded by a razor-sharp pendulum. Surely the mind that conceived such wickedness was more responsible than the actual perpetrator. It was time to see that the Dark Invader got his just rewards.

"Eleanor Dalton!"

Eleanor? Mother hadn't been angry or scared enough to call her that in years. Nelly's feet paused briefly, but certainly not long enough to apologize for her disobedience. She was too busy trying to catch up with her brother in dress shoes that pinched.

Nelly overtook her brother and Quinlan in front of the brownstone house. A single cellar window was barred, and the cellar door under the front stoop was bolted from the inside, but the coal chute wasn't. Quinlan was too broad to fit. Fitz handed his tie, celluloid collar, and suit jacket to his mother. "Sorry about the dress trousers, Ma," he whispered, "but it can't be helped."

Dorothy Dalton had accepted defeat valorously, to join her children in their folly. Eyes smoldering behind their glasses bespoke punishments to come, however. Fitz's own eyes shot between his mother's and the gaping blackness of the waiting hole. At the moment, the hole seemed safer.

He began lowering his long frame, feet first, into the opening, then stopped as an operatic soprano voice warbled through the air from the house. Fitz glanced up at Quinlan. "Sir?"

"Remember your father's notes about the German opera singer? Wagner." Jim grinned. "Brünnhilde's big moment. And just in time. That racket will cover anything. Hurry, while she's still inspired! Oh, and here. These might cast a little light on the subject."

Fitz deftly caught the proffered box of matches and disappeared amid a cloud of soot. Huddled beneath the steps, Mrs. Dalton silently prayed while Quinlan followed the music and Nelly kept her eyes on the bolted entranceway.

Fitz seemed to be gone forever. When the *skreek* of the opening basement door came, it would have cut the night—but for the bellowing still emanating from the second floor.

Fitz's head poked out. "You're not going to believe this," he whispered excitedly. "The cellar looks almost like the laboratory set from Episode Fourteen. I'm sure they've been making those bombs here! And the funniest thing, Ma?"

"What, Fitz?" Fear made her answering whisper even softer.

"All that stuff you made up about inoculating animals with germs?"

There was a pregnant pause.

"Rows of vials are just sitting around, marked with things like 'E' and 'B cultures.' "

"Real evidence at last! Come out of there, Fitz," Quinlan ordered, his voice low but firm. "At once! Shut the door and hide behind those cans—all of you. I'll be right back."

Cowering behind garbage ripe from standing too long in the city's heat, the Daltons caught—over the soprano's final, frenzied strains—the unmistakable sound of a nightstick firmly striking a nearby pavement. Secret Service agent Quinlan was summoning the only troops he could muster—New York City's finest. The police.

Nelly put an arm around her mother as polite applause drifted from the second-floor salon's open windows. "I'm truly sorry, Ma," she murmured. "Fitz and I really got you into this one."

"Speak for yourself, Sis. You didn't have to follow."

"You know I did, Fitz. I was sick and tired of being the fragile, helpless heroine. But now there'll be police, and reporters, and—"

Dorothy Dalton's shoulders stiffened, almost setting

the garbage can behind her toppling. "I'm fed up with hiding, children. Maybe this was necessary. Maybe we'll really be able to bury your father and Black Tom once and for all."

Dorothy Dalton's words were barely spoken before the cavalry arrived in force. Seemingly in seconds, the street and house were silently cordoned off. And in the thick of the activity was Agent Quinlan, directing everything. He certainly looked as if he was having fun. He'd borrowed a megaphone from the police and now commenced barking into it as decisively as Holmquist on a movie set.

"Occupants of 111 West 15th Street. You are surrounded. Come out with your hands high!"

Rescued from their odiferous sanctuary, the Daltons stood behind the line of policemen, waiting with curious neighbors for the denouement of the drama. One by one, figures emerged from the front door. First was a very large, buxom woman gowned in silks. Brünnhilde herself.

Nelly nudged her brother. "She forgot to take off her headdress. Golly, but she looks ridiculous with those cow horns sticking out!"

Fitz snickered. "And there are the gents who were dining with Panther. They don't look so confident now."

"But where is Panther?" Nelly scanned the building from roof to basement. "The basement, Fitz! There's a flicker of light through the window . . . The evidence! He's going to burn the evidence!"

"Don't be silly, Nell. Jim sent a cop down there. Didn't he? . . . Nell?" Fitz twisted around to where his sister should have been. Gone! He glanced back at his

mother, enwrapped in the drama, then ahead. That must
be Nelly, ducking under the police line. Fitz nipped off
in pursuit.

A trickle of smoke met Fitz at the basement door. He
ran through it. Nell was right. Someone *was* trying to
destroy the laboratory. Could it truly be Paul Panther?
Charming, debonair, funny Paul Panther? "Nell? Nelly!"

Fitz groped through the first room, trying to remember
it as he'd seen it earlier by the light of Jim's matches.
There'd been a work sink, with water for the experiments.
He was sure of it. He stumbled over something. A
bucket. Good. Couldn't let all that evidence go up in
smoke. Fitz found the sink and opened the water valve.
Just before the trickle turned into a flow he heard the
sounds—in the next room, the laboratory room. The
room with the growing glow of light.

"Nelly?" The bucket clattered over unheeded. Water
spewed forth in a deluge. Fitz ran. He halted dead in his
tracks at the open door.

"Panther. Even *you* can't be that evil!"

Paul Panther, serial star, had one arm twisted tightly
around Nelly's neck. His free hand was busily groping for
a syringe, poking it into one of the vials marked "B cul-
ture."

"Why not? It's because of the Dalton twins that I need
a hostage. All my years of careful work, careful acting,
have been unmasked by you two *amateurs*! *Amateurs,*" he
spat out again, as if it were the worst epithet he could
think of.

Nelly managed to loosen the hold on her throat for a

split second. "We are *not* amateurs! Only wait for the first reviews of our serial—"

Fitz couldn't wait. The smoke was thickening; tongues of flame were coming perilously close to tables filled with explosive elements; Panther's hand had almost filled the syringe with deadly poisons. Fitz dove for the Dark Invader's legs.

15

Closing the Net

Getting a stranglehold on the Dark Invader at last, Fitzhugh Dalton unmasks the archfiend moments after saving his sister Nelly from the cauldron of acid. Gasping with disbelief, they see before them their guardian, Paul Panther. Lieutenant Lloyd Wright and the police are summoned. Panther is led away growling imprecations and revealing yet another reason for his treachery—as their guardian, Panther was due to inherit the Dalton Family Fortune should the twins meet an untimely death. A satisfactory ending to an above-average serial improved by its imaginative screenplay and introduction of the crowd-pleasing Dalton Twins.

—"This Week at the Serials," *Moving Picture World*

Nelly was slowly removing books from their makeshift cases and shoving them into storage boxes. "I can't believe I'm standing here, Fitz, calmly packing after last night. After that, that *archfiend*—"

"—Your friend and mine, dapper Paul Panther, alias Captain von Rinthoven, alias the Dark Invader—the Kaiser's own Master Spy—throttled you and nearly pumped you full of deadly bacteria?"

Nelly tentatively touched the black-and-blue spots on her neck. "They're real this time. Panther's genuine fingerprints. Thanks for saving me, Fitz. Just in case I forgot to say it."

"You didn't forget, but all thanks and praise accepted

nevertheless. It's rather nice being appreciated for my true heroic, valiant, and stout-hearted self." Fitz dodged Nelly's carefully aimed book, grinning. "Watch out for my bruises, Sis. I picked up a few in that flying tackle, too."

Despite the hot Sunday afternoon, Nelly shivered. "Thank goodness Mother spotted us going through the police lines and sent Jim after us. Only another few minutes and that entire house might have blown sky-high."

"In an explosion that only Cedric Holmquist could have properly appreciated."

Nelly pulled out a handkerchief and swiped at her damp brow. "Speaking of whom, I'm not at all sure how we're going to get through the last week of shooting. Without Panther and all."

"Don't worry, Sis." Fitz was fondling the violin case. "If necessary, Holmquist will cart the camera right into Panther's jail cell to get those last shots."

Dorothy Dalton stopped her enthusiastic pecking at the typewriter nearby. "How *do* you suppose Jim is doing with Panther? And all those others that were captured? It certainly seemed as if a whole nest of German spies were meeting in that house last night."

Fitz yawned. "A noisy lot, too. That opera singer yodeling for attention, and the others yelling for 'bail'—just imagine expecting bail, all the time they were trying to destroy our American way of life!"

Nelly packed the German dictionary. "I guess Jim will be too busy for a while to come and tell us."

Fitz brightened. "Maybe we'll read about it in the papers tomorrow."

"I'm afraid not, dear," his mother answered. "*We* may have been finally ready to meet the reporters, but the government had other ideas. The whole business comes under top-secret classification. Our country is still at war, after all."

"Then we won't be heroes!"

"Only in the serial, Fitz." Dorothy Dalton attacked her keys with a satisfied smile and renewed zeal. "But the information won't be classified forever. And when the lid comes off, I'll have the first, true-life story of the entire Dark Invader affair ready for publication!"

Holmquist was not happy Monday morning. "First Schmidt gone, now Panther." He turned on Lloyd Wright. "And our noble lieutenant threatening to sign up for the real War this very afternoon in a fit of misplaced patriotism."

Lloyd stood very straight and tall within his fake uniform, suddenly the consummate, idealistic young officer. "I can't in conscience wait any longer. Not everyone is a Benedict Arnold like Panther. Someone has to even the scales, Cedric. Someone has to keep the flag flying."

Nelly felt a wonderful thrill of pride travel down her spine before Holmquist continued his ranting.

"Save me from jingoism! It isn't fair! How am I supposed to finish this serial?"

"Shoot Lloyd's final scenes first," Nelly tried. "And surely you have some random close-ups of our guardian's face, Mr. Holmquist? If they could be cut in—"

"Better yet," Fitz suggested, "the audience needn't see

Panther's face at all. Just our looks of horror and outrage
. . . Titles could fill in the rest."

"Hum." Holmquist fiddled with the lens around his
neck and took two paces. "The final ignominy. To
be betrayed by one's own guardian . . . one's father
figure!" Holmquist was warming up to the idea. "To be
left total orphans, the unwilling masters of your fates.
Pathos. *Bathos* even. To have to eke out a new life from
nothing . . ."

"Well, there are a few million dollars in the bank, pre-
sumably—" Fitz interjected.

"—not to mention the Estate," Nelly concluded.

"But on studying the Estate books, you learn that Panther has drained it all away, into some secret account of
the Central Powers. And the Estate itself has been dissi-
pated, is no longer yours." Holmquist had forgotten
Lloyd Wright and was circling the twins, more and more
excited. "You will be left nothing. Not a single golf club
or tennis racket! Nothing but the clothes upon your
backs, and a burning desire for *revenge*!" Holmquist's face
turned beatific. "What a glorious point from which to
begin a new serial!"

"We didn't have the heart to tell Cedric we were going
back to school next week, Ma. Not with Lloyd enlisting
and all."

Mrs. Dalton was heaping stew into their bowls for dinner. "It's going to have to be done, Fitz. I found a little
place for us in Manhattan today, and gave Mrs. Bernini
notice . . . The last scenes for Episode Fifteen have been

turned in. There's no more work for me here, and I can write my true-life story, *Beyond Black Tom,* just as easily across the Hudson."

Fitz bit into a dumpling glumly. "Everything is turning so *ordinary* again. I'm not sure I can stand it." He chewed slowly. "And it all seemed to begin with Dad's shopping list. Dumplings and cigars . . ."

The apple tree behind Fitz's back rustled, but only Fangs seemed to notice. There was a low growl from his throat as he tried to heave himself from underneath the table past Fitz's legs.

"Fangs, what in the world—"

A thick, scarred face poked through the window, followed by a gun-wielding arm.

"You will make dog to halt. Now!"

Nelly's eyes went as wide as in her most dramatic serial scenes. "Schmidt! But you're in jail!"

"No longer." The rest of his body struggled into the room. "It was not comfortable. Neither convenient. Also I am much upset by you terrible *Kinder.*" His gun seemed a very large one, and it was pointed in turn at each of the Daltons.

"Where to begin with gun shooting? I have wanted bad to do this for much time."

Dorothy Dalton had been clutching her throat, but finally got out a word. *"Why?"*

"Your husband, he catch me at Black Tom performing Panther's orders. I get away, but I spy on him. See him make notes. I search him before throwing him to inferno. Nothing . . . This evidence must be found. When I first track you from New York, I hear most interesting words from outside window, words which bring you too close to truth. But I am discovered." He shook his head regretfully. "Then I think: If *Kinderschwein* are eliminated, and mother . . . who is left to know?"

Fangs was choking himself trying to get at Schmidt, but Fitz hung on. "Sorry, boy, it would delight me to let you at him again . . . but he does have a gun." Fitz's words were much calmer than his demeanor. Here was the true villain responsible for Black Tom. Responsible for his beloved father's death—even if Schmidt had merely been working under Panther's orders. His knuckles turned white as they gripped the dog.

"Yes." Schmidt smiled grimly. "I have gun. Big gun. Many bullets. Soon are you all finished. *Kaput.* And my work continues. Even without supervision of Dark Invader. Such pleasure it will give me to end you . . . Every time I am seeing stupid Black Tom badge being worn like jewelry I am also seeing red, am almost losing control—"

Nelly's eyes narrowed as she clutched at her brooch. "The bear hug . . . They'll catch you, Schmidt. They'll catch you and hang you."

"Not before I blow up many more things. First studio. Bigger bombs this time. I destroy all films against Germany. I destroy entire serial! Never will it be seen. Never will its lies be spread across country. Then more factories, more ships—" He stopped himself. "Too much talk. Now action."

Nelly watched Schmidt's finger begin to tighten on the trigger. "Only answer one more question, Mr. Schmidt. Before, before you . . . Please."

He hesitated. "What?"

"How did you knock me into the mud at Black Tom, without getting any on yourself?"

Schmidt grinned and his trigger finger relaxed. "Very clever, yes? And simple. All my idea, too. Not Panther's, like avalanche! I wait until you cannot see me, then remove trousers, shoes, even socks. I wade out and—" He made a shoving motion with his hands. "It was most uncomfortable trip back, however, with mud on legs and toes."

"Poor Mr. Schmidt. The Kaiser should be saving an Iron Cross for you."

"Yes!" His grip on the revolver tightened once more as he clicked his back ramrod stiff. "Most certainly Iron Cross after I complete business of tonight. For the Kaiser!"

Schmidt aimed directly at Nelly. She held her breath, watching Fitz's shoulder slowly rise toward the saboteur's gun arm, Fangs being released—

She ducked as the gun went off. Simultaneously the door to their apartment crashed open. Fangs had Schmidt's gun arm between his teeth before another, separate shot ran out.

"Don't move, Schmidt. The next bullet won't be a warning!"

"Jim!" Dorothy Dalton flew at Quinlan. "How did you know!"

Quinlan shrugged her gently away. "Duty first, Dory. Some fool at headquarters turned his back on this one while I was out. I figured he'd return to the scene of his crimes. Like I said, all brawn and no brains."

Fitz was gingerly examining Schmidt's gun as several agents followed after Quinlan to complete the subduing of Schmidt. "Maybe I'd better hang on to this, in case somebody lets Panther out—"

Quinlan held out his hand for the weapon. "Sorry, Fitz. Evidence."

Holmquist was almost beside himself on the final day of shooting.

"What? You're going back to school? With the whole world ahead of you in pictures? You'd give that up? You'd give up the new contract I just negotiated for you, too? Star billing!" He waved some papers before the twins' eyes. "Right there at the top of the screen! Bigger credits than Panther or Wright ever had. The contract spells it out in black-and-white! And bigger salaries! I even had them throw in an automobile as a bonus—"

"What kind of an automobile?"

"Fitz." Nelly tugged at her brother's arm. "Fitz. We have no place to keep an automobile in Manhattan. And you know we have to finish school, then college—"

"But you have natural talent, both of you. What a waste!"

"I thought you were trying for California, Mr. Holmquist." Nelly's attempt at distraction worked.

"Perhaps next year. By next year they'll be begging for my services, and you can come with me—"

Sam the cameraman had been watching the whole scene through his lens. "Stick with school, kids," he hissed. "Cedric sent film samples to Mr. Griffith and never even got a reply."

Dreams of owning an automobile slowly faded from Fitz's eyes. He walked up to Holmquist and held out his hand. "It's been educational, sir. Thank you."

Nelly followed suit. "Every time someone tries to drown me or bury me alive, I'll think of you, Mr. Holmquist." She glanced at her brother. "We'd better get home to our packing, Fitz."

"If we must . . ." As a sudden thought struck him, Fitz turned back to the director. "Sir?"

Holmquist's distraught expression turned hopeful. "Yes, young Dalton?"

"Might that automobile still be available next summer?"